SISTERS' SECRET

Cort Fernald

Publisher's Note: Sisters' Secret is a work of fiction. Names, characters, places, and incidents are a product of the author's imagination. Locales and public names are sometimes used for atmospheric purposes. Any resemblance to actual people, living or dead, or to businesses, companies, events, institutions, or locales is entirely coincidental.

Thanks to S.H. for invaluable assistance with editing and formatting. Thanks also to Nebraska Writers Workshop and Torri Pantaleon.

Library of Congress Control

Sisters' Secret/ Cort Fernald. -- 1st edition
ISBN 978-0-615-98313-4

For my wife, sister and brother-in-law

"Don't get too far ahead, Georgie," the bushy white haired man called, shading his eyes from the low sun of early morn. He smiled, watching the burly boy run down the field to a copse of grey leafless trees. Georgie ran with such joy, his arms waving overhead, thick legs churning and red coat flying behind him like a cape.

"Ah own't Gamps," the boy yelled back.

"Don't lose your mushroom bag." Gramps liked to take Georgie mushrooming when he wasn't on a serious foray, like spring morel season. The boy didn't know lichen from velvet foot and usually spent the day filling his bag with puffballs. Gramps had to go through Georgie's bag to make sure he didn't pinch and pick a death cap or other poisonous mushroom. Bundling his black and yellow Iowa Hawkeyes sweatshirt tight against the autumn chill, the old man thought it a perfect day for a hunting Chicken of the Woods or Hen of the Woods. Not a mushroom but a fungus and in season. Washed, sliced, Hen of the Woods was delicious pan fried in olive oil and garlic.

Georgie loped along the tree line atop the steep embankment that led down to a creek. "Hen? Hen?" He liked to call out as he searched. You wouldn't know the boy was 19 years old and, as Gramps often said, didn't have all his buttons. He had the innocence, curiosity and sweet disposition of a child half his age. Gramps preferred a world full of Georgies than most people.

Walking was difficult for the old man and he struggled to catch up to the boy. "Found any?"

"Uh ahhhhhhh." Georgie turned and gave Gramps an open mouth and wide-eyed look.

"Gotta keep looking." He reached the trees. "Look under fallen logs or brush and leaves. The damp spots." Gramps poked at some leaves under a bush with a stick.

With darting birdlike movements of his head, Georgie watched Gramps and then imitated him switching a stick under the scrub brush. He bent low, losing his balance, pitching forward and tumbling down the embankment. "Gamps!" he cried out, crashing through dead leaves and spiny twigs to the creek below.

"Georgie? Georgie, are you okay?"

Silence.

"I okay, Gamps."

"I can't come down there with my bad leg. You're going to have to climb up on your own." Gramps could hear Georgie breathing hard and thrashing around the brush. "Can you do that?"

No response. Then Gramps heard Georgie suck in a breath. "Uh oh...uh oh..."

"What's the matter?" The old man held onto a tree branch and carefully lifted his leg over the embankment. "I'll try and get as close to you as I can."

"Hen, Gamps," Georgie said, starting up the dense growth of the embankment.

"Here, I'm right here. I'll pull you up."

The boy scrambled through the tangle of thicket and up the embankment. He got near and lunged for Gramp's outstretched hand. Pulling and pushing, Gramps managed to get Georgie out of the wood and over the embankment.

"Are you okay, Georgie?" Breathless, the old man said, "You really scared me when you took that header."

"I okay," the boy said, holding up his black mushroom bag. "Hen."

"What?" Gramps chuckled. "I'll be darned. After all that, you found some Hen of the Woods. Good boy. Here, lemme see."

"No. Ah hen." Georgie shook his head and half-turning, pulled the bag back.

"It's okay. I just need to see it." Gramps reached out. "That looks like a big one in your bag." Slowly, Georgie turned back and handed the black bag to Gramps. "It's heavy too." He opened the drawstring and started "Ahhhhhh." The bag fell to the ground and out bounced a hand. A human hand, severed at the wrist, lay on the frosty ground. It was a small hand, a left hand with the third finger torn off and splintered white bone sticking out.

"Hen," Georgie nodded.

"Oh my god," the old man said. "Is that what you found down there?"

Georgie pointed down to the creek. "Uh huh..."

"We have to call the police." Gramps pulled his phone out of his sweatshirt pocket.

The boy crouched down and intently stared at the contorted hand with his head tilted to the left, then tilted to the right. "Uh oh...uh oh..." He didn't seem to understand.

"911? My grandson and I were out mushrooming and found a hand down in the creek." He listened. "Yes, a human hand. Oh, it's Jordan Creek in Raccoon River Park, near the baseball fields. Yeah, I mean the softball complex." Georgie reached out for the hand. "Georgie, don't touch it. What? Yes, it's definitely a human hand and small, like...Oh God...like a child's or woman's hand." Gramps bent over and examined the hand. "There's some kind of writing, or red letters carved on it." He stood. "Okay, we'll wait." Gramps clicked off the phone. "We have to wait for the police. They're sending a patrol car."

"Peese car? Peese man?" Georgie's face lit up, excited.

An older, heavyset black man in a silver Lands End down jacket stood in the middle of the field, drinking coffee from a pink pig-shaped travel mug, well back from the activity behind a line of yellow caution tape. He watched with no expression on his round face. A crime lab van and patrol cars with blue and red lights flashing parked haphazardly in the field on either side of the stand of trees. Uniformed officers and crime scene investigators in white coats bustled up and down the embankment. A tall middle-aged white man in a heavy olive drab parka scrambled through the underbrush, slipping but managing to climb the embankment. He spotted the older man and walked up the field.

"Chopped her up pretty good, Stokes," he said, leaning over, swiping at the leaves, twigs and dirt clinging to his pant leg.

"Yeah...I saw," Stokes replied, staring forward. "How long you been here, Evans?"

"Since the call came in they found a body by the creek." He stood up. "I could use a cup of coffee?"

"Finish it," Stokes handed Evans his mug. "Did we get an ID?"

"Ain't I special," Evans took the mug and drank. "Yeah, Millman found an ID."

"Millman?"

"New guy," Evans pointed to a younger man in a tan trench coat hunched over with his hands on his knees between two patrol cars. He was taking deep breaths.

"What's the matter with him?"

"He went down to the creek to see the body—puked his guts out."

His mouth twisted sideways, Stokes shot Evans a sidelong glance.

"Hope the crime scene boys don't bag up his barf as evidence."

"Her purse was empty. Girl shit like makeup and tampons scattered all over. Wallet was tore up. No credit cards, driver's license—but Millman found an old Southern Illinois University student ID."

"Where'd he find it?"

Detective Evans shook in a silent laugh. "Right next to the bush he was throwing up on."

"What's her name?"

"Rebecca Devereux on the student ID," Evans explained. "Attractive gal. And we matched up a 911 call that came in two nights ago from Mike Smith, West Des Moines address, reporting his wife Rebecca D. Smith missing." He tipped the pig mug, took a swig and spit it out. "All the sugar's at the bottom."

"A lot like life, innit? It ain't sweet until nearly gone." Stokes said. "Did we pick this guy up?"

"Couple of cars went and got him. He should be at the station."

A uniformed patrolman, with Gramps and Georgie trailing, walked up to the detectives.

"Looks like gramps got a hitch in his get-along," Stokes mumbled.

"The 'tard and the old coot want to know if they can go now." The patrolman poked his thumb over his shoulder, looking to Stokes then Evans.

"The what?" Stokes said. Evans raised his hand in front of Stokes.

"I mean the older gentleman. They want to know if they can go."

"Did you get a statement? Names? Addresses?" Evans asked.

"Yeah...but it's weird. The 'tard keeps saying he wants the hand. The hand...the hand...the lady's hand he found."

Gramps' overheard them.

"He can't have the hand," Stokes said. "That's evidence. This isn't finders keepers."

"I think you're misunderstanding," Gramps spoke up. "Georgie's not saying *hand*, he's saying *hen*."

"Hen? Like a chicken?" Stokes glanced at Evans, who held up both hands like he wanted no part of the conversation.

"Yeah, Hen of the Woods," Gramps replied.

"You're out here looking for chickens?"

"No. It's a fungus that's in season."

"A fungus?" Stokes stared, baffled. "What do you do with it?"

"Eat it...like a mushroom. You fry it and it's really tasty."

Evans lowered his head and raised the pig mug so Gramps wouldn't see his face contorted in laughter.

Stokes stood silently looking at Gramps. "Enough of this. Patrolman, thank this gentleman and his grandson for being good citizens and escort them from the scene."

"Will do."

"And patrolman...I want to see a certificate that you completed the department's sensitivity training on my desk next week...or you'll be busted to bikes for the rest of your life."

"Yes sir." The patrolman hustled over to Gramps and Georgie and led them away.

"Wonder what he calls me behind my back," Stokes muttered.

"No way am I taking that bet."

"Who wants to eat fungus? You want mushrooms...you go to Hy-Vee. You don't go rooting around the woods finding dead bodies."

A gaudy blue van, with long boom and satellite dish on the roof and TV station logo splashed on the side, pulled up, stopping in the softball complex parking lot.

"Uh oh," Evans murmured.

Stokes glanced over his shoulder. "Damn it." He turned back. "Hey... Millman!"

The young detective looked up, wiping his mouth.

"Get up there and keep them god damn TV people away."

Millman nodded and waved, running across the field while holding his stomach.

"Well," Stokes said. "Let's get back and see what kind of actor this husband is."

"Academy award performance, maybe..." Evans replied.

"Like hell," Stokes grumbled, trudging back to the parking lot.

1

A large disco ball spun, hung from the high ceiling shooting light like falling stars over all the walls.

Mike stood in the shadows, off to the side of the entrance to the Holiday Inn convention hall, reluctantly peering in the dark ballroom. An amateur band clamored through *Train in Vain* on a small stage across an expanse of tables and lighted dance floor. A crooked crepe banner above the stage had hand painted green lettering reading Rich High Class of 1979. Welcome Rockets! Welcome Rockets Conference Champs Baseball.

These were the children of the GI Bill, plopped in a cornfield under Phil Klutznick and Elbert Peets' grand design of rolling meadows of affordably priced ranch-style homes, the tail end baby boomers of Park Forest, Illinois; whiter than white, the upwardly mobile of the middle class, the straightest of the straight arrows, those privileged and suburban. It was the doctors' good work: Kinsey, Spock and Seuss. They had turned out as planned, just like Park Forest, cookie-cutter same, moral and proper Republican offspring. At least, at first glance.

Flecks of light whirled round and round.

"Hey, Mike Smith," a voice called from behind.

Mike turned but didn't immediately recognize the man and woman walking toward him.

"I know it's been quite a while," the stocky man said, holding out his pudgy hand. "But I can't have changed that much."

Mike stole a glance at his nametag, smiled and said "nope, you haven't Bill...Bill More." He took his hand and they shook. "I'm sorry—I remember you having quite a bit more, um," Mike touched the top of his head. "And it was red if I recall."

Bill laughed and patted down the thinning strands combed over his balding head. "I remember that too." Bill motioned to the woman standing next to him. "Mike, this is my wife Edie."

"Very nice to meet you, Edie," Mike said, shaking her hand. Edie was a smallish woman, rounded in all the womanly places. She wore her red hair cut short, pixie-style which suited her ruddy chubby features. Her expression changed to motherly concern as Bill expressed their condolences.

"We heard about your wife Becky, and want to offer our deepest sympathies. A terrible crime. Simply awful."

Listening, his head slightly bowed, Mike crossed his hands in front, touching the heavy gold band on the ring finger of his left hand. "Thanks. But how did you hear?"

"You need to keep up with your classmates," Bill said. "I've been senior editor of the Park Forest Daily for more than twelve years now. It came over on the AP wire."

"Oh, I guess you would've heard then."

"Did you come alone?" Edie asked.

"Yeah," Mike replied quietly.

"We're meeting some people from our group," she added. "You're welcome to join us at our table."

Bill and Edie started to move toward the door.

"That's very kind of you," Mike said. "I might stop by. It was good to see you Bill, and nice to meet you Edie." And they disappeared into the dimly lit ballroom.

Thank you Mike thought, spoken more in courtesy and habit than any real appreciation. My wife was repeatedly raped and brutally killed, thank you for acknowledging that; thank you for reminding me she's gone. Thanks for bringing back those haunting images of her body in the morgue—her body laid out like puzzle pieces on the stainless steel table; her head hacked off at the neck, her blue bruised and ashen grey face drained of blood with those beautiful brown eyes fixed in terror. Thank you so much.

The West Des Moines police had pushed him around and showed him graphic pictures during the interrogation. The husband is always the first one suspected. It wasn't his emotional breakdown seeing his wife's dismembered body but witnesses' verifying Mike was at work in his company's Rockford, Ill. call center at the time of the abduction that disappointed the cops.

Other couples passed through the entrance. Mike half-smiled, self-conscious. He didn't recognize anyone. Picking at the collar of his grey button down shirt, pulling at the sleeves and smoothing over the lapels of his black suit coat, Mike slipped into the ballroom darkness. He took a breath, letting his eyes adjust to the ballroom dim. Tables surrounded a dance floor. Off to the side at the bar, lines of people in small clusters with drinks in hand, conversed and listened and nodded and laughed. Couples filled the tables around the dance floor. There were empty tables in the back.

Driving in from Iowa until the moment he pulled into the Holiday Inn parking lot, Mike debated whether to go to this reunion or turn around. His life had changed so much since his wife had been killed six months ago. He thought getting out might keep the images of her mutilated body from playing endlessly through his mind. He tried not to think and just kept working and going home to a silent and empty house. It was difficult, but he needed to get out, to get back in the swim. He let out an audible sigh that got the attention of a woman walking past him. She gave him a quizzical look. He weakly smiled in reply then made his way over to the bar and shuffled into the queue.

"Make way...look out, man" a boozy voice called out.

Mike spied him right off and tried to look away. It was Donnie Inge with two beer bottles in each hand and shouldering his way between the lines. He came up to Mike and stopped with mouth agape.

"I'll be goddamned, it's Smitty," he said. "I never thought I'd see you back in Park Forest."

"How are you, Donnie," Mike replied. He didn't need to ask how he was; he was well past drunk.

"I got a table over there," Donnie said, nodding. "C'mon."

"Let me get a pop," Mike said.

"Hey," Donnie offered. "I got an extra—C'mon."

"Thanks, I can get one of my own."

"Naw, no way," Donnie started to nudge Mike out of the line. "You're not going to ditch your ol' right fielder, are ya?"

"Give me a second," Mike said. Frowns and narrow eyes followed him as he slid to the front and asked for a soft drink. "Okay, let's go," he said, following Donnie as he weaved through the tables.

Ma ma ma...ma Sharona, the singer wailed.

People at tables glanced up at Mike and he nodded whether he remembered them or not. Donnie had a table across the floor along a side wall. There was no one else at the table. Mike pulled out a folding chair and watched Donnie's unsteady collapse into a chair.

"Here by yourself?" Mike asked.

"Yeah," Donnie said, tilting his head back and taking a long drink. "Got no bitch giving me any shit tonight." And he laughed.

"Yeah, I'm on my own too."

"We all heard about your wife," Donnie said, sounding less than sympathetic. "Drag isn't it?"

Mike regarded him for a moment, not knowing how to take his comment; then decided to acknowledge it in some way. "Thanks. I guess a drag is a good way to put it." He took a short drink. Donnie had always been tactless.

"Well, to my way of thinking, you're a free man now," Donnie said brightly.

Taking a deep breath and forcing a smile, Mike thought, how can I get away from this guy? "Hey? Is Coach Picolo here?"

"Coach Peaches? Naw, he ain't here. You've been gone a long time, man. Ol' Peaches got killed in a hunting accident, ten or fifteen years ago."

"What? I was hoping to see him."

"If you do he's a ghost. He was hunting with Rod Decker, his dad and bunch of other people. Coach wandered in between a rifle and a buck. There went Peaches, drilled in the back of the head."

"I'm surprised," Mike said, almost to himself. "Coach hunted all the time. He knew how to take care of himself out in the field. What was he doing with the Deckers? He hated the old man."

A couple walked by. "She got fat," Donnie said, getting a dirty look from the woman as she passed.

He surveyed the room commenting on the grown up members of the Class of '79. "I thought that guy died of AIDs," he added. "Wow, look at the tits on her. I don't remember that chick having knockers like that in school. Maybe she had a boob job? Hey, check out those two. They've been together since high school." He laughed with a guttural sound in the back of his throat, a malevolent laugh.

Mike glanced around also, noticing some people staring at him. Was it because of Donnie's loud voice or did they all know about his wife? This was a bad idea. And now he was sitting with Donnie. He wanted to leave.

"Looky there, it's Grace House?" Donnie reached out, grabbing Mike's shoulder. Mike turned in his seat. Coming in were a couple, a petite woman with dark hair and a taller man. "You used to go out with her, didn't you?"

It was indeed Grace who Mike had dated in high school. "Yeah, we dated for a while. Then we broke up."

"She was fine, man. Nice ass." Donnie said, leering. "Didn't she ditch you?" Mike shot him a look, annoyed. It made Donnie chuckle as he tipped the bottle to his lips.

"You heard the story didn't ya?" He sounded as if telling a dirty joke. "The rape? She was raped...big time."

"What? Grace?" Mike repeated in disbelief.

"Yeah, man," Donnie said, swallowing, sighing and wiping a line of white foam from his upper lip with his sleeve. He was slumped forward, braced by his elbows on the paper cloth covered table. He squinted trying to focus his red-rimmed eyes on Mike. "She was snatched and raped." Donnie said slowly and emphatically. "Her little sister Chastity too."

"What are you talking about?" Mike said, his tone rising. "Who did it?"

Donnie swayed and looked at Mike for a minute. "Wha'do you care, Smitty? You weren't going with her anymore."

"You're lying."

Donnie smirked. "You got what you wanted."

"That's a lie," Mike shot back.

"Whoa, dude, easy. It was a long time ago. Who gives a shit?" Donnie finished off his beer.

"Maybe I give a shit," Mike said loudly, over the band. Donnie looked away at couples getting up from tables and filtering through the colored lights to the dance floor.

Mike jumped from his seat and went over to Donnie. Donnie tipped back startled.

"Who did it?" He said into Donnie's ear, emphasizing each word. "I want to know."

Donnie nearly lost his balance, but Mike grabbed his suit jacket collar and jerked him upright. Donnie's expression changed to fear and confusion. "Hey," he squealed over the music. "I thought we were friends, man. I don't know. I don't know shit. Lemme go."

With a shove, Mike let loose of Donnie. Friends...with him? He wouldn't have put it that way. You go through little league, American Legion, and high school baseball with a teammate you think you know. You think you know their secret story, but not really, not enough to be friends.

"We've known each other a long time, Smitty," Donnie brushed down the front of his jacket. "Man, Smitty, I didn't even call you Shitty...Shitty Smitty," and he chuckled.

His lips tightly closed, Mike exhaled through his nose. Didn't take long for that nickname to come up, he thought. "Shut-up, Donnie," he said.

"Shitty Smitty. Shitty Smitty," Donnie chanted, grinning.

It reminded Mike of the locker room taunts from the seniors when he was a sophomore. He could feel his heartbeat racing, but kept his composure.

"Awright. Awright," Donnie said, struggling to stand. "I'm getting another beer. You want one?"

"No, I'm fine," Mike said, leaning back in the folding chair.

"Oh yeah, I forgot. You drink pop." Donnie walked unsteadily through the tables to the bar at the back of the ballroom.

Mike's classmates had become quite well-rounded, especially the jocks and the cheerleaders. A lot of the spiky hairs were short and thin-hairs, and the tie-dye was a summer blazer with open collar polo shirt or a simple print full figure dress. He recognized a couple of people, and some of the cliques had reformed for their own reunion. Surveying the people he realized there were no black or Hispanics in the entire class. Then he remembered Park Forest was predominantly white when he was growing up. It wasn't until the mid-seventies that minority families started moving into the suburb. A poignant incident from when he was a boy came back to him. One of the first black families to move to Park Forest bought a house up the street from Mike's house. People weren't happy about it. Mike didn't understand. It was just another family. Nor did he understand when the owner of the house next door to the black family painted their side of the fence black and his side white. Mike understood that, the irony of southern-style racism in the middleclass suburbs of Chicago. It reminded him of Mark Twain's comment, if you want to eliminate prejudice, travel the world.

"Gotcha a pop, man," Donnie said, spilling the cup as he set it down. Swaying, he nearly fell into the chair.

"Thanks," Mike said, taking a sip. He grimaced and nearly spit it out.

"Ha!" Donnie laughed. "C'mon, loosen up, have a drink. It's party time. Most of these old broads are hot to trot."

Mike pushed the drink to the center of the table. He looked at Donnie and wondered what had happened to him. His hair was sparse, grey-streaked and missing in patches. His face was worn, pasty and sagging. He had a bright red open sore at the corner of his mouth and another on his chin. He was dressed in a wrinkled cream-colored suit jacket with an out-of-date skinny black tie. Jeans and dirty running shoes completed a look that seemed more down and out than careless cool. He hadn't gained much weight on his bony frame, but for the round belly he carried over his belt. He'd always been ill-kempt and that hadn't changed.

"How come you didn't bring a girl?" Donnie asked. "What're you, gay?"

"No, I'm not gay," Mike impatiently replied.

"I don't remember—did your wife die?"

Mike recalled that Donnie would take any drug any time, available or if he could steal it. Once Mike pulled into a gas station and saw Donnie surrounded by a bunch of kids. He had his nose stuck into the gas intake, breathing deeply. He reeled back from the tank, let out a loud whoop and climbed back into the driver's seat.

"No," Mike said battling the music. "She was killed."

"How'd ya get away with it?" Donnie chuckled, holding the beer bottle at his lips.

You asshole, Mike thought but said nothing.

"Just kiddin', man."

"What about you? Where's your wife?" Mike replied sharp.

Donnie threw his head back, laughing so hard he almost fell over. "Which one?"

"Oh," Mike weakly smiled. "How many wives have you had?"

"Three! Three fuckin' bitches!" he answered half in glee, half in spite. "Three ball bustin' bitches!" The music stopped and 'bitches' echoed across the ballroom. Heads turned toward them.

The nastiness of Donnie's tone made Mike uncomfortable.

"One bitch is in Texas, or Mexico, I don't remember. No idea where the second one is—and damn happy about that! The third is in Chicago Heights, not far enough away she can't get right up my ass with her spike heels."

"You got kids from these holy matrimonies?" Mike couldn't resist slipping in sarcasm.

"Couple...boy and a girl, I think. Don't know where the hell they are now. 'Course, they don't know where the hell I am, so I didn't have to pay any child support."

"Lucky you," Mike added.

Vice Principal MacLemore slowly and with some difficulty, hobbled across the stage. Years had withered away his imposing physical presence. Skeletal thin, in an ill-fitting sports jacket, the stage lights gave MacLemore's face a ghostly grey pallor. He appeared much less the than the fearsome authority figure stalking the hallways when Mike was in school. MacLemore was now tasked as the host of the class reunion. He took the microphone from the singer. "Before we open the buffet," he croaked and cleared his throat. "We have some announcements." He paused, shielded his eyes and looked into the crowd. "Behave yourself, Mister Peiper. I can still put you on detention." A gentle giggle rippled through the crowd. "We have members of the conference champs and almost state baseball champion Rich High Rockets here tonight and we will bring them up after dinner." A cheer went up from a crowded corner table. "But right now—let's eat." He held out the microphone to the singer. The singer talked to the drummer. MacLemore dropped the microphone. Boom! Laughter, scattered applause and electronic feedback filled the ballroom amid the scraping of chairs and noise of people getting up for the buffet.

"I'm getting something to eat. You coming?"

Donnie's mood changed, brooding, reminded of his wives and kids. "Naw, you go ahead. I'll catch up with you later."

"Suit yourself. You need to eat something."

Mike moved through the tables to the buffet where a line formed. People smiled and nodded and he responded with a smile or nod, even though he had no idea who they were. Did they all know about his wife's murder or remember him as a ball player in school? Such a bad idea, he repeated to himself.

Hands in pockets he joined the buffet queue. Knots of cliques and snobby groups had reformed along the line. A group at the front surrounded a tall, paunchy man with tinted, shiny, hair the color of ox blood penny loafers. The tall man squinted at Mike with a searching look, then broke out in a wide grin. Mike recognized him, Mr. Popularity himself, Rod Decker.

"Hey, it's Shitty Smitty!"

People turned. Mike faintly smiled, quietly replying. "How are you doing, Rod?"

Rod took long strides up the line, his hand outstretched. "No hard feelings."

"No...but do me a favor." Mike took and shook Rod's beefy hand. "I'm 48 almost 49 years old...isn't it time to put away that childish nickname? Call me by my real name."

"Oh, come on, Sh---alright." Rod flashed a stretch of perfect white teeth, the smile that set girls hearts aflutter. "What the hell is your name?"

"Mike."

"I knew that. Heh...heh...heh. Mike Smith, Rich High's best third baseman. I never thought I would see you at one of these shindigs."

"I needed to get out of the house."

"Heard you were working over in Somalia, Vietnam or some buttfuck place like that."

"I've been working on and off in India and England for the last couple of years."

The line moved forward.

"India? You been taking our jobs? Heh...heh...heh."

Mike had forgotten Decker's irritating monotone laugh, mirthless and hollow.

"No." Mike shifted his weight. "What about you, Rod? What've you been doing for a living?"

"Well, ball didn't work out. So I went into construction, and then real estate. Things are going real well these days. You never heard of Rod Decker Realty? And my Pop wants me to run for state assembly next year. Hey, you can vote for me."

"I live in Iowa."

"This is Illinois...that don't matter. Heh...heh...heh."

Rod had an oversized block shaped head with wide forehead and elongated jaw. His once strong athletic build had gone south and expanded east and west. He knew it and tried to cover his gut with a double-X Hawaiian print shirt, untucked. Creased beige golfer-style leisure slacks and white patent leather loafers completed his look.

"Rod! Rod!" a slightly overweight woman in a too tight, too short dress cried out in a raspy voice.

"Hey. That's my girl. Remember her?" Rod motioned to the woman. "Sherry Leaway? The cheerleader? Which way? Any way; Leaway goes all the way. Heh...heh...heh."

"Oh yeah," Mike replied, smiling at the woman. Her face puckered like she caught a whiff of a bad smell. "That your wife?"

"My wife? She ain't my wife. Heh...heh...heh." Rod gave Mike a nudge with his elbow. "What about you. Where's your Missus?"

"She's not here," Mike said softly.

"You're not one of them..." and Rod trailed off, giving Mike arched eyebrows.

"My wife, um, passed away last year," Mike said, wondering why some people think you're gay if you're not with a woman.

Rod feigned a right jab to Mike's stomach. He hunched over bringing his hands up to protect himself. "Well, looks like you're keeping yourself in decent shape."

"I work out and still play ball...softball."

"You do?" Rod seemed surprised. "I work out too," he added with a twisted smirk. "I put my feet up, switch the ball game on TV and do 12 ounce curls. You still look like that guy in Risky Business or somebody like that. Heh...heh...heh."

"Rod! Rod!" Sherry's rasp went to shrill.

"Better get my ass back up there," he said. "Good to see ya. Take care of yourself, Shitty...ahhhhhh, I mean...Mike." He waved as he moved up to the front of the line, taking a plate and joining his group going down the buffet. They clustered around him, casting glances back at Mike, whispering and gesturing.

Mike stepped along, taking a plate and utensils. People seemed to give him a wide berth. He stabbed at a couple of slices of roast beef and put them on his plate and moved on to the next dish. Filling a plastic glass with ice and water, Mike turned back toward the ballroom.

He wasn't sure at first, then realized ahead of him were Grace and her husband. What Donnie had said about Grace being raped came back to him. She seemed changed, but in many ways looked the same as in high school. Short, with a trim waist and short auburn hair, Grace was dressed conservatively, perhaps a little overdressed with a sweater and long skirt for summer. The man she was with, that Mike presumed her husband, was of average height, with brownish hair with some grey streaks. Neither handsome nor plain looking, what struck Mike was how protective he seemed to be of Grace. She was skittish moving through the crowd and clung close to him. He ushered her out. Noting her husband's solicitousness, Mike became aware of people parting in front of them. Women darted disparaging looks at Grace and pulled their husbands aside.

Mike wanted to talk to her. Yes, she had broken up with him though Mike never knew why. He hesitated.

Mike watched Grace and her husband zigzag through the chairs and tables to a setting in the back of the ballroom. It didn't appear anyone else sat with them.

On an impulse, he followed.

"Mind if I sit with you?" he asked.

Grace putting down her plate and drink, looked up startled.

"Not at all," her husband said.

Grace shot him a look. He flinched and tried to back track. "I...I mean," he stammered, "if it's okay with you, babe?"

"It's fine," she said under her breath, sitting.

Mike set his plate and glass across from them.

"Hello Michael," she quietly said.

"Hello Grace."

"You two know each other?"

"This is my husband, Jeff...Jeff Jordan," Grace said. "Honey, this is Michael Smith."

Mike stood, reaching across the table to shake hands. Jeff half rose and hastily shifted the fork to his left hand.

"Nice to meet you, Michael."

"You too, Jeff. Please, just call me Mike."

"Since you know each other," Jeff wondered aloud. "Should I worry that you're an old boyfriend?"

Grace shyly smiled.

"We dated," Mike explained, sitting, unfolding his napkin. "We dated through summer and our senior year."

He carved a square of beef and paused. "That was a long time ago. What would you say, Grace?"

"Sounds about right," she carelessly said. "We went to a lot of concerts, school functions and I can't tell you how many baseball games Michael dragged me to." The subtle trace of a smile crossed her face.

"So I shouldn't worry?" Jeff said, almost joking.

There was a long silence.

"Oh no," they both finally said and laughed.

"Baseball games?" Jeff exclaimed. "How in the world did you get her to go to a baseball game? She won't even watch sports on TV."

"I played on Rich High's baseball team."

"Michael was the star third baseman on the school team. All Conference, second team."

Mike stared at his plate.

"The team they're honoring tonight," Jeff started, with a mouth full of food.

"Yeah," Mike nodded his head. "Two errors and one out away from going to the state championship."

"Jeff went to New Trier High," Grace said.

"That Rich High team was good," Jeff added.

"We had good pitching, good infield and outfield and some clutch hitters." Mike leaned back, staring into the dark above them. "But something was wrong with a couple of our key guys in that last game. They were out of it. The shortstop and our first baseman, Rod Decker, made uncharacteristic errors. And Donnie Inge, seemed totally out of it. Those guys were out all-night partying or stoned or something. We were better than that Centralia team." Mike's eyes came back to Grace. "Oh yeah--and the morning of the game I get a call from my girlfriend dumping me."

"That didn't stop you from hitting, three for four with a double," Grace said meeting his gaze.

"How did you know that?" Mike asked his fork halfway to his mouth. "Were you there?"

Grace's oval face had matured handsomely with small lines around her green eyes and at the corners of her smile. In the random flashes of light from the mirror ball, Mike could see the face of the teenage girl.

"I don't want to talk about any of this," Grace quickly interrupted, her hands in front of her as if to ward off danger.

Mike and Jeff exchanged glances.

"Are you okay?" Jeff asked concerned, looping his arm around her.

"Grace, I'm sorry," Mike said. "It was a long time ago."

Grace took a deep breath and calmed down after a few minutes. "It's okay, Michael. I just...just...didn't want to hear about a baseball game or other stuff from back then."

A couple walked past and Grace waved. The tall blonde woman noticed Grace's wave and gave her a polite, if dismissive nod. They didn't stop.

"Who was that?" Jeff asked.

"Rachel. She used to be my best friend."

That was how it was for Grace in high school, Mike remembered. The months they dated people talked to Grace and it appeared in all ways normal. After she broke up with him, classmates shunned Grace. At the time he believed people were being sympathetic to him.

They ate in silence for a while and Mike wondered if he should excuse himself. But he gathered the courage for another try talking to Grace. "So...what have you been up to, Grace?"

She sighed thoughtful, dabbed her mouth with the napkin, replaced it on her lap and said, "just raising kids. We have two. I'm working part time in a law office and tending my garden."

"Don't forget Mabel," Jeff reminded her.

"Oh, yeah," Grace said. "Taking care of our little baby, Mabel."

"Baby?" Mike exclaimed. "You've a baby! That's great."

Grace laughed. "Yes...Mabel is our baby, our big baby. We have to constantly take her on walks or she'll sulk. So we have to spell everything out because if she hears the word *walk* she starts jumping and running around in circles. Then all she wants to do is play with her toys...and she has them scattered all over the house. She won't leave the cat alone."

"Wait?" Mike was confused. "Walks...running around in circles...the cat?"

Grace giggled louder. And Jeff smiled broadly.

"I thought you had a baby named Mabel," he said.

"We do, Michael," Grace said, reaching over and touching his arm. "Mabel is our four-legged barking baby."

"Oh, you had me going," Mike chuckled.

"I know," Grace said. "I was having fun with you."

Mike was relieved the conversation had turned back onto a friendly tack. "What do you do for a living, Jeff?"

"Me?" Jeff swallowed hard and cleared his throat with a drink. "I'm a tool and die man, manager of Illini Tool and Die in Chicago Heights. Been there for almost thirty years...and I am really looking forward to retirement."

"And your kids?" Mike asked.

"Our oldest girl Chas is working at a marketing firm in Chicago. Chase just graduated and is working with Jeff at the shop. We're not totally empty nesters. I still have loads of laundry to do on the weekends."

"Two boys?"

"A girl and boy."

"Chas?"

"Short for Chastity."

"You named her for your sister. That's cool."

"Yes," Grace said quietly, her eyes shifting away. "What about you?" She added, taking in a breath.

"I've a grown son, Spencer. He lives in Renton, Washington and works for a software company. He..." Mike hesitated, glancing down. "He and I have some issues."

"Sorry to hear that."

"Oh, we'll get it sorted out," Mike said, feigning a carefree attitude. "I hope," he couldn't stop himself from adding.

They went quiet again and this time Jeff picked up the conversation. "So, Mike," he asked, wiping his hands on a napkin. "It's your turn. What do you do for a living?"

Mike, glad for the shift in topic, said, "I'm the Call Center Director for Data and Research, Infobyte Group. We're based in West Des Moines, which is where I live."

"I've heard of Infobyte," Jeff said with his mouthful. Grace ate and listened, looking from Jeff to Mike. "Don't you have a call center in Rockford?"

"Yes," Mike warmed to the subject. "Also call centers in Gurgaon, India and Manchester, England."

"Do you travel a lot?" Jeff had his elbows on the table, his hands folded under his chin, curious.

"Pretty much...I can do a lot via ftp, email, phone or over the computer, but I have to do some traveling at least twice a year. I don't mind," he added. "I enjoy traveling."

"Traveling alone? I heard you married, right?" Grace asked.

"No," Mike replied slowly, his head tipped to the side, wondering if perhaps Grace did not know about Becky's death?

"Divorced?" Jeff questioned.

"Watch out, Michael," Grace said, glancing at Jeff. "If you're single Jeff will try and set you up with his sister."

"Oh Hon," Jeff laughed.

"No," Mike somberly said, raising his head. "I'm a widower. My wife died about six months ago. She was the victim of a crime." He took a breath. A wave of sadness welled up inside him. He was getting choked up. "I'm sorry. I haven't got over it, yet."

Grace and Jeff stared at Mike in silence.

"I must sound like a total loser," Mike said. "I should go..."

"No!" Grace said, reaching out and gently putting her hand over Mike's. "No, it's our fault for asking."

"You didn't know."

"Don't go," there was a strong emphasis in Grace's voice. Jeff gave her a pat on the shoulder. "We are very sorry to hear it," she added.

Mike watched Grace, in the back of his mind remembering what Donnie had said about her and her sister being raped. How could something that horrible have happened to her? Something stirred emotionally inside as she talked.

"Mike?"

"Oh, I'm sorry," he said.

"You were lost in thought," Jeff added.

"Yeah, I guess I was."

"If it's not too personal, Michael, how did your wife die?" Grace asked.

Mike paused weighing whether to defer the question or tell Grace and Jeff the truth. If he deflected it would just bring more questions. It was difficult to summon the courage but he decided to tell them. "I wasn't truthful when I said she died," Mike confessed. "She was...was," he sighed deep. "...raped and murdered." Mike dropped his eyes. Again the images of his wife Becky's naked, dirty, bloody, mutilated body came swarming into his thoughts. They had cut off her arms and hacked off her legs and sliced off her breasts and cut hateful words into her flesh: whore, slut, cunt. Those horrible words were nothing compared to the horror seeing a large anarchist star the killers had carved on her back. The cops had shoved him against the wall, called him a murderer, sicko, rapist, pervert, scum; then pushing him into a chair and inches from his face, yelled he'd get death for killing his wife. "I didn't do it," Mike repeated over and over through his tears.

Mike looked from Jeff to Grace and chose not to elaborate, sparing them the gruesome details. He could barely contain his emotions as he spoke. "They raped her," he hissed, through clenched teeth. "Again and again. Killed her and then cut her up."

Grace gasped, a hand to her mouth. She tried to disguise her response. Mike saw it.

The conversation throughout the ballroom grew to a loud hum.

"I'm, I'm so sorry," Jeff murmured. "Did they catch whoever did it?"

"No," Mike replied.

"There the fuck you are," Donnie staggered up, with beers in hand. "I thought you were coming back to our table."

Strangely, Mike was relieved with Donnie's interruption.

"I saw Grace and her husband and wanted to say hello." He motioned over to Grace. "Grace, you remember Donnie?"

Grace turned away, toward her husband. Her face was screwed up in an angry expression. She wouldn't acknowledge Donnie.

"Grace?" Donnie snickered low, taking a swig of beer. "I remember you."

Something was off and Mike didn't quite understand. Did Grace know of the ugly rumors Donnie had been spreading about her? "And this is her husband, Jeff," Mike said, gauging Grace's reaction.

Jeff offered his hand to Donnie. But Donnie held up the beers and shrugged his shoulders.

"Nice to meet you, Donnie," Jeff politely said.

"Likewise, man," Donnie said. "I'm headed back to our table, Shitty. See ya over there later." He stumbled around then turned back. "Real good to see you too, Grace," and chuckled to himself as he weaved away.

Grace turned on Mike. "Why are you hanging around with that piece of trash?" Grace said accusingly.

Surprised, Mike studied Grace a moment. "I didn't recognize too many people when I got here, except for Donnie. I just kind of sat with him."

"And why do you let him call you that...that awful name?"

"Was he swearing at you?" Jeff put in.

"Sounds like it, doesn't it," Mike said.

"What did he call you?" Jeff innocently asked. Grace shot him a glance, then looked back at Mike and lowered her head as if to say sorry she he had asked.

Mike drank the last of his water, and explained wearily. "They call me Shitty...Shitty Smitty. It rhymes...sort of."

"That's a bad nickname."

"You want to hear the story?"

"Not if you don't want to tell me," Jeff said.

"It was also a long time ago."

"You know the story, Hon?" Jeff asked Grace.

"Yes."

"Well." Mike took a breath. "It started when I was a sophomore. Some of the guys like Donnie and Decker would chew during ball games. I never could sit during a game, so I would pace the dugout when we batted. I walked past one of those guys just as he spit. The spit landed on the back of my white baseball pants. The other guys saw that and thought it funny. They began to spit brown tobacco juice on the back of my pants as I paced. It became a big joke. I had no idea what was going on. This went on for a couple of innings. I was getting the strangest looks from players on the other team. I went up to bat and the umpire called time and as he brushed the plate whispered to me asking if I needed to use the restroom. I had no clue why he asked and said, no, I was okay. It wasn't until after the game, at my locker, taking my pants off, that I held up my pants and the whole back was covered in brown stains—it looked like I had crapped my pants. That's when the whole locker room burst out laughing. Decker yelled out...that's real shitty and someone else said, pretty shitty Smitty. And they started chanting Shitty Smitty Shitty Smitty. From then on I was known as Shitty Smitty."

"We all have high school trauma," Jeff chuckled. "But that takes the cake."

Grace slapped his arm. "It's not funny, Jeff."

Mike snorted a little laugh. "It's okay, Grace. He didn't mean anything by it. It's so long ago it no longer stings. Now it just seems silly."

"And they still call you that?"

"Some guys do. It's mostly the ones that like to needle me," Mike said.

"I remember playing softball one time and our left fielder made this fantastic running diving catch and he," Jeff couldn't stop himself and started to giggle. "He gets up, throws the ball in and runs straight off the field. I yelled out. Hey, where you going? He yelled back..." Jeff cupped his hands around his mouth and said "I shit my pants." He broke himself up laughing.

"Jeff!" Grace exclaimed.

Mike grinned, just for that moment he felt carefree and easy. Jeff and Grace's interplay reminded him of intimate moments he and Becky had shared. He missed her so much. It wasn't fair. Watching them Mike found it hard to comprehend. Why would Grace be snatched and raped? He could hear Donnie's voice saying 'repeatedly raped'. She was never a tease, nor what they called easy. She didn't dress provocatively. When she and Mike dated they had made out and petted as it was called back then.

But they didn't have sex. Why did they think he and Grace had had sex?

"Michael?"

He had had the reputation for being a ladies man and getting any girl he wanted. High school reputations are not always the truth.

"Yo...Mike?"

Was the rapist someone who knew Grace and her sister and figured she was loose because she and Mike had dated? He couldn't bear it if in some way he was responsible for what had happened to Grace and her sister. He realized he had a lot to ask her. Maybe she would know what Becky went through in those last few minutes. And then his own son Spencer thought he was responsible for his mother's rape and murder. The day of the funeral, with the closed casket, Spencer sat next to his father, saying little. He looked so much like his mother that Mike had a hard time not seeing Becky in his features and not breaking down. Spencer stood stiffly throughout the ceremony, staring ahead with a cold and set expression. As they lowered Becky's casket into the deep rectangular cut in the ground Mike reached out for Spencer. But his son stepped away.

"Mike?" Jeff and Grace were snapping their fingers at him.

He started.

"Are you alright?" Grace asked.

"Oh...I'm sorry. I was miles away."

2

Mike left the reunion as vice principal MacLemore called to the stage members of the conference champion baseball team. He had no desire to climb the stage into the spotlight. Mike said his goodbyes to Grace and Jeff, traded phone numbers, and promised they would get together again—soon. Before leaving, he went over and found Donnie sitting alone with his head supported by his arm on the table. He shook him vigorously, faked sincerity, and said it was good to see him. "Sure thing," Donnie said, lurching toward the stage hearing his name called. As Mike walked out, he glanced over at Grace, hoping she looked after him. She and Jeff were engrossed in their own conversation.

The drive back to West Des Moines clocked in close to eight hours with a lot of time to think. Mike thought about Donnie and what a waste his life had become. Not just the four wives, but the kids, the drinking and no steady job. Mike remembered him as a very good ball player, a multi-tool outfielder. "Hey Donnie Clutch" they used to shout from the bench when they needed a hit. He delivered. All Donnie ever wanted to do was play ball. But his after game celebrations started to go long into the night and weekend. Soon it was pre-game hair of the dog. And the drugs. They were all over in those days. Donnie couldn't resist. Mike was no angel, though he didn't smoke, drink or pop pills during baseball season. Well, he corrected himself, he liked them greenies.

Pro scouts looked Donnie over; and some division one colleges extended scholarship offers. By the end of Donnie's senior year, it was iffy whether his girlfriend, a freshman, would have the baby before or after graduation. Decker had started a betting pool. Then there was the little matter of a minor in possession getting jail time or community service. No one was surprised the college recruiters stopped coming to games. All but one major league scout had pocketed his notebook and left the field. A stint in the army didn't help. Dishonorably discharged weeks after joining, Montreal did sign Donnie on the word of one scout and after he got out of county jail for domestic abuse, he hopped a bus to an instructional league team in Sonora, Mexico. Mike lost track of Donnie after that, except for a short sports item in the newspaper with a picture of Donnie being escorted from the field by Federales. He started a fight—not with the other team, but with his own teammates.

As the miles stretched west on I-80, Mike's thoughts wandered back to Becky, though he tried his utmost not to. It hurt too much. "I miss you," he whispered over the engine noise, as he looked out at the headlights lighting the dark road ahead.

And Grace? Jeff looked like a good guy. If he went by appearances alone, they looked to be in a loving marriage.

Grace and Mike hadn't been a serious item in high school. They dated, went to outdoor concerts in Grant Park, to Comiskey Park for White Sox games, a homecoming and prom—mostly it was the occasional A&W snack and a movie. They weren't hot and heavy as others were at that age. But then, the morning of the clinching game at regionals she called and said they were over. Mike was shocked and a little sad, but it wasn't heartbreak.

The way Donnie said it seemed like everyone thought they had done it, and so the rape of Grace and her sister was par for the course. That's probably why people seemed to shun her in school and at the reunion. Mike's anger boiled up again. He hadn't known anything about Grace being raped and learning about it now made him feel badly for her, not having been there when she needed him. The same feeling he had not having been there for Becky. That sarcastic comment from Donnie that he shouldn't care because he had got what he wanted enraged him.

Who did that to her? What kind of animal does that to women like Grace and Becky and countless innocent women? Why? What kind of sick society do we live in? How can you be proud to be a man? Is this how it always will be, every man an animal? It wasn't for the pleasure of sex, but to subjugate, dominate and control. He glanced into the rear view mirror and saw his eyes in the darkness. Quickly he looked to the road ahead. He felt shame and responsible for what happened to Grace. Whoever raped her and her sister Chastity must have thought them easy prey. And Becky, was it someone that knew her or knew Mike? Was Spencer right that he was responsible?

Mike reached the outskirts of Des Moines. He promised himself to contact Grace the next time he was in the Chicago. He had to talk to her. She would understand how Becky suffered. Mike needed to know her last moments.

Mike's phone beeped. He didn't recognize the number on the screen. "This is Mike."

"Mr. Smith?"

"Yes," Mike hesitantly replied.

"It's Detective Millman, West Des Moines Police Department. I wanted to call and give you an update on the investigation into your wife's...death."

"Have you caught whoever did it yet?"

"Mr. Smith...we are actively pursuing all leads, but I am sorry to tell you that we...ah...haven't apprehended any suspects yet."

"You have any leads?"

"Well..."

"Then why are you calling?"

"J-just...to update you. We've some DNA tests still being analyzed by the state crime lab. We might get a hit on the hair and..." he paused. "And the...ah...semen...semen samples. Once we get the results we can see if there's a match on the national...sex offenders' database."

Mike listened in silence.

"Mr. Smith?"

"I'm here," he responded, almost under his breath.

"We'll...touch base again once we get the test results and maybe," he said brightly, "a match."

"Okay."

"Talk to you soon, Mr. Smith" Millman said. "Have a nice...um...good-bye."

It took all of Mike's strength to flip on his turn signal and brake the car, pulling off the interstate. He gripped the steering wheel tight and dropped his head.

Freckles. Mike had never been attracted to girls with freckles, but there was the most fascinating girl standing with another girl in the order line in front of him at LaRoma's Pizza. She looked around, bopping to Depeche Mode on the pizzeria speakers. Mike was almost certain they were SIU students also. Noticing Mike watching her she broke into a shy smile, her cheeks coloring.

He returned her smile and said "hi." She turned away, embarrassed, just as he was about to introduce himself.

It must have been her disarming smile, but Mike had to meet her. She wore her lush black hair up with thick strands falling to her shoulders framing her oval face, in stark contrast to the blow dry look of the day. Her bangs were over her eyebrows almost in her eyes and those large hazel eyes were made up discreetly with mascara accentuating the lashes. But it was the scattering of freckles across the bridge of her narrow nose from cheek bone to cheek bone that captivated Mike.

He tried to catch her eye as she and her friend took their order from the counter and went to a table in the crowded dining room. Her friend gave Mike a sidelong glance. But she didn't look, nor smile.

She wore white jeans with a black and white checked pullover. The pullover didn't have the big padding in the shoulders like the trendy girls wore. Tall, slender, she carried herself with a careless elegance.

"Welcome to LaRoma's Pizza," voiced the bored teen behind the counter dressed as if in Culture Club. "Whud'll it be?"

"Oh," Mike started. "Two slices of pepperoni with extra cheese and a coke." Pepperoni? "No, wait. Can I have sausage instead?"

"Extra cheese?"

"Yeah. Extra cheese and a 7up. Thanks."

"For here or to take away?"

"Here."

"It'll be a minute."

Mike waited on his order, glancing around to see if there was a vacant table near where she sat. There wasn't. He weaved through the students and families and set his tray on a table. He unslung his book bag. She sat in the corner talking and nibbling a slice, She flashed a look in Mike's direction. He spotted her and grinned. He wasn't hungry anymore, but took a bite and pulled a heavy textbook out of his bag and opened it. He couldn't focus to read and every so often glanced up from the blur of the page to see her. She was. Trying to act nonchalant, Mike smoothed the wrinkles out of his black Public Image Ltd Flowers of Romance T-shirt and patted down his hair. "I hope she doesn't think I'm the grubbiest looking guy on campus," he thought.

Talking to her girlfriend, they got up to leave. Mike stood as they approached.

"Hi," he said, blocking their way. The two stopped, a bit surprised. "Aren't you in my econ class?" he asked quickly, all but ignoring her friend.

"I don't think so." An awkward silence followed.

Mike panicked, not knowing what to say next.

"But I've taken econ," she finally replied. She noticed the open textbook on the table. "Did you need some help?"

"Yeah. Yeah, if you have a second?" Relieved, he motioned her to a chair.

"See you back at the house, Becks," her friend said, walking away.

"Okay, Tiff," she said.

"Your name is Becks?" Mike said as they both sat.

"Oh no," she smiled. "It's Rebecca Devereux...but I hate that. People call me Becky or Becks."

"My name's Mike, Mike Smith. Are you from Carbondale?"

"Please," she giggled, twirling a long strand of her hair in her fingers. "I'm from Schaumburg. You?"

"Park Forest," Mike replied. "What's your major?"

"Business Administration, third year. What're you studying?"

"Computer Science."

"And you have to take econ?" Becky turned the text book around, reading.

"Yeah," Mike said. "It's a real drag."

The opening guitar riff and Latin jazz rhythms of Style Council's *You're the Best Thing* played through the pizzeria.

"Mike," Becky said in a serious tone, fixing him with a gaze from her hazel eyes. "I see your problem right here." She tapped the textbook with her white fingernail.

"Yeah? What?" He leaned over, concerned, his eyes flicking from Becky to the text book, to Becky.

"This is a psych book," She said sternly. "If you're studying a psych book for an econ class you're headed for an F."

Mike said nothing. Becky regarded him suspiciously. Then she burst into laughter, rocking back in her chair and clapping her hands in front of her face.

"Busted," he confessed. "I just had to meet you, Becky."

"That's sweet. It's nice to meet you too, Mike."

"Ah, I was wondering if," he stammered. "Well, if you were seeing anyone?"

Becky cocked her head and brushed aside the bangs from her eyes. Mike smiled, his eyes open wide and brows upraised. "I am seeing someone," she responded.

"Oh," Mike said, crestfallen. "I didn't mean..."

"I'm seeing a really nice and cute guy named Mike," she interrupted, crinkling her nose. "This Friday, if that's okay with him."

His face lit up.

"Where shall we go, Mike?"

You're the best thing that ever happened...
To me or my world...
You're the best thing that ever happened...
So don't go away..."

Freckles, Mike thought. What he wouldn't give to see her freckles right now.

3

Weeks after the reunion Mike tried to contact Grace.

"Hello?" a male voice answered.

"Hi, is this Jeff?" Damn, Mike thought. He hoped Grace would answer.

"Yessssss?" he said slowly, with some suspicion.

"This is Mike, Mike Smith...from the reunion?"

"Oh, Mike...how ya doing?"

"I'm well. Hey, I'm traveling though Chicago next week and I thought the three of us could get together for lunch...maybe..."

Jeff paused. "Next week?"

"Yeah," Mike said. "Thursday or Friday. I have a layover in Chicago."

"Mike...I'm sorry. We would like to see you as well, but I am going to Michigan to see my grandkids next week."

"I guess maybe some other time then." Mike was disappointed.

"Hold on. Hold on, Mike," Jeff added. "I won't be here, but Grace will. Hang on." He covered the phone, but Mike could hear him call out.

"Grace?"

"What?"

"Mike wants to take us out for lunch next week."

"Who?"

"Mike. That friend of yours from the reunion?"

"Oh, Michael, yeah. But you're going to see the kids."

"I know, but why don't you go to lunch with him?"

"Me?" Grace asked. "Why me?"

"His wife...remember? He's probably pretty lonely."

Mike's head dropped. He wanted to hang up at that moment.

"Oh yeah," she said. "Okay. Tell him I'll go to lunch with him."

Jeff came back on the line. "Hey, Mike," He said in a happy tone. "Grace will be here and she said she would love to have lunch with you and catch up on old times."

"Thanks, Jeff." Good, good, Mike thought. "Tell Grace thanks and I will give her a call next week when I get into town."

"Sounds great," Jeff responded.

"Have a good trip to Michigan," Mike added. "Bye."

"I hope to. Thanks. Bye" Jeff ended the call.

Mike sat quietly a moment, his hand on his forehead, wondering if he did appear to be 'sad and lonely' to others.

He telephoned Grace the following week and suggested they have lunch at a small cafe in Homewood. Grace agreed. Mike listened closely; there didn't seem any hesitation in her voice.

Mike arrived early to the Greenleaf Café, a small boutique type café on the main street of upscale Homewood. He was nervous. In the months since his wife's murder he'd gone on a couple of arranged dates (by well-intentioned co-workers and relatives) and internet web site coffee setups. They had all turned into a disaster with women excusing themselves and fleeing out the back door, or being motherly and suggesting he seek counseling. He knew Grace was married and happily so. But he couldn't help the memories of how they would kiss and clutch when they dated in high school. He'd been respectful of her boundaries. When she said stop, Mike did. These thoughts would drift across his mind. He would have to snap himself back to his senses. A part of him felt ashamed.

Inside the Greenleaf Café he waited while a young blonde in a starched white shirt, black skirt and apron came around the high glass front deli case at the back.

"Table for one?" She asked with a big smile.

"No," he said with a tinge of pride. "I'm waiting for someone."

"Perhaps in the back?" She motioned to an empty table in a far corner.

"Ah, no," Mike said. "This table in the front would be fine." He pointed to a table in the corner, bathed in sunlight through the large café window. "That'll do."

"This way, please."

Mike followed her and took a seat with his back to the wall. She laid menus in front of Mike and the opposite setting.

"Would you like something while you wait?"

"Coffee...with cream," he added as she walked away.

The café was half-filled, mostly with middle-aged women lunching with other middle-aged women, a couple in casual work attire and a pair of young girls working on laptops. He self-consciously realized he was the only solo in the café. Since his wife's murder, he'd been alone in everything he did. The coffee came, with a handful of plastic 'cream' packets strewn in the middle of the small table.

Mike finished his second cup of coffee when he saw Grace step from a large sedan parked across the street. She wore a sundress with a yellow pattern, beige canvas flats and her hair looked as if she had just left the beauty parlor. Mike tried to suppress the thought about how pretty she looked. She spotted the café, shouldered an oversized brown handbag, and started slowly across the street.

Grace entered the café.

Mike stood and signaled to her.

The blonde came from serving a far table and followed Grace.

"I'm so glad you came," Mike said. He held out his hand.

"Of course," Grace said, shaking his hand. She dropped her large bag with a sigh on a chair, smoothed the back her dress and sat across from him. "Did you think I wouldn't?"

"I didn't know if you would. I'm glad you did."

"Hello," the girl said. "Would you like something to drink, coffee, tea, soft drink?"

"I would. Thank you."

"I didn't mean I thought you wouldn't. It's just..."

"Since it's too early for a glass of wine, iced tea with lemon would be fine," Grace said as an aside to the girl. "It's just what, Michael?" She added.

"I'll get that for you," the blonde said and left.

Grace turned back to Mike.

"We haven't seen each other in more than thirty years and this is the second time we've seen each other in a month," he said. "Besides, we didn't get much of a chance to catch up at the reunion." Mike laughed lightly and Grace smiled, opening the menu.

"Though, if we see each other next month my husband will start worrying," she mentioned in an offhand way.

Mike smiled and toyed with his coffee cup.

"What's good here, besides the coffee?" she asked, waving to the coffee cups collected in front of Mike. He had to laugh again. It felt good to be teased by a woman.

"I don't know," he said. "I have never been here before."

"Do you mind if I have dessert instead of lunch?"

"Grace, you can have anything you want."

She made a coquettish face and scanned the menu. Mike was charmed. He told himself he would have to rein in his emotions or he might make a fool of himself. They were quiet studying the menu.

"I am," Grace finally declared.

"You are?" Mike asked.

"I am going to have dessert." And she closed the menu and slid it to the side of the table.

"Well, I'm a little hungry myself, so I think I will have a cup of onion soup and a salad." Mike, gently mocking Grace, closed the menu, slapped it on the other menu and folded his hands under his chin.

"You're hungry?"

"I am," he deliberately said. "But I am very glad you came."

"Again with the glad I came," Grace chided. "Michael, Jeff enjoyed meeting you at the reunion. So having lunch and catching up is perfectly natural."

Mike considered whether to tell Grace how difficult it had been for him since his wife's murder when the blonde girl came to the table.

"Are we ready to order?" She placed a tall glass of ice tea, with a slice of lemon split on the rim before Grace.

"Yes, I think we are," Mike replied, motioning to Grace.

"Me? Okay," Grace said. "I would like a slice of your New York cheesecake with raspberry topping, and just a little dollop of whipped cream."

Mike grinned.

"Okay," the girl said with a faint smile.

Pleased with herself Grace sat back.

"And you, sir?"

"No dessert for me," Mike said. "Not just yet. I would like a cup of onion soup and a small salad."

"What kind of dressing on the salad?"

"Ranch would be fine."

"Another cup of coffee?" she asked.

"Yes, please." Mike looked across at Grace as the girl turned on her heel. "Dessert? I thought you were kidding."

"Is there something wrong with that?" She knew he was teasing.

"No...not a thing."

"Are you saying I'm fat?"

"Oh my, no. You are not fat at all." She wasn't in the least. Grace had the curves of a middle-aged woman, but not out of proportion.

A phone buzzed in her bag.

"It's Jeff." She fished through her large bag. "He said he'd call when he got to Michigan."

"Excuse me," Mike whispered and rose.

He found the small restroom and stood above the single toilet. Staring at the wall he realized how much he missed the nervous excitement when in the company of a woman. Washing his hands, Mike looked in the mirror and saw red-rimmed eyes with dark semi circles underneath. If only he could get a good night's sleep and not lay there alone in the dark remembering Becky and thinking of Grace.

Grace was still on the phone when Mike returned and sat. She ended the call and put the phone on the table.

"Jeff says hi and hopes we all can get together when he gets back."

"That's a good idea," Mike replied.

"But what I want to know," Grace said, her hands on the table between them. "...is how you are?" Her voice lowered to a sympathetic tone. It was the tone people took when talking to him just after his wife's murder. Mike had come to hate it.

"I'm fine," he responded matter of factly.

"No no no," Grace said, shaking her head side to side and narrowing her eyes at Mike. "Tell me the truth. How are you?"

He couldn't fool her. The earnestness of Grace's question and expression took Mike by surprise. "Wh-what do you mean?" He fidgeted with his wedding band.

"You know what I mean, Michael," she replied. "Since your wife's murder."

The girl came up with coffee and placed it on the table, taking away the two empty cups.

Mike took a deep breath, looking out the large window and sighed. He didn't expect her to ask that. He needed a moment to compose himself. Grace shook a paper packet of sugar, tearing off a corner and pouring it into her ice tea. She stirred the tea and ice cubes jingled. Mike looked back at her. She held his gaze unflinchingly, waiting on his reply. Mike remembered how they had always been able to talk, with nothing out of bounds.

"It's been...rough," he said, clearing his throat.

"And it was..." Grace hesitated. "A murder and...rape."

"Yes," Mike poured cream from the plastic packs into this coffee, adding sugar and stirred slowly, thoughtfully.

"How did it happen?"

Mike stared at the swirling coffee as he answered. "Becky was a manager at Conestoga Bank in West Des Moines and worked late one night. I was in Rockford at the call center. It was dark when she went to her car in the parking lot. There were two flat tires. The..." Mike stopped. "The surveillance cameras...the police showed me the surveillance videos...showed her calling on her phone. She was calling me to come pick her up. I got the call but was in Rockford. I was just too far and told her to call Triple-A. In the video you can see a black car come up quickly. Three men jumped out. They pulled Becky from her car and forced her in their car." For a long while Mike was silent, staring out the window. The sound of the ice in Grace's tea brought him back. "You could see her fight them. But they overpowered her. On my way back I called and called. She didn't answer. I had a horrible feeling in the pit of my stomach. I just knew something was wrong." He drank from his coffee. His hand shook. "It was two or three in the morning when I got back to West Des Moines and the parking lot of the bank. Becky's car was still there. The driver's door was partly open. I remember I saw her phone on the floor of the driver's side. Something terrible happened to my Becky. I called the police. She'd disappeared."

"I'm sorry, Michael" Grace said, pausing. "You don't have to tell me anymore."

"No," he said. "I want to tell you. I have never told anyone what happened that night. People ask what happened. They don't really want to know."

"They probably don't want to make you relive it," Grace took a sip of iced tea.

"Or they can't bear hearing it," Mike said. "You, Grace, you can bear hearing it. You understand."

She searched his face, questioning.

"Two days after that night an old guy and his grandson found Becky's body in Raccoon Park in a wooded area. Well...the grandson found her hand. They had hacked her body to pieces, arms and legs and left it by a small creek. Her head was severed and her...her...sex, was cut out." Mike's hand went to his face and he wiped tears away. Grace offered a cloth napkin. "They had raped her repeatedly then mutilated the body. The cops took me in and just grilled me. They were sure I did it."

"I'm sorry, Michael." She said, her voice quivering. "And...your son?"

"Spencer?" The question took Mike aback.

"You said at the reunion you had a son...was he there with you?"

"He came a few days after, for the funeral," Mike said distantly. "He was upset. He thought I had left Becky in the parking lot...left her alone there."

"The murder must've hit him hard."

"I've tried to talk to him. I have apologized for what happened. It's like a wall between us."

"It'll get better, Michael. You have to give him time."

"What about me, Grace?"

They were quiet.

"Grace," Mike said, turning his coffee cup on the saucer. He took a breath and said "I wanted to see you to catch up with you, not talk about my sorrows."

"I'm sorry," she said earnestly said. "I thought it would help you to talk it out."

The blonde came up with plates. "Onion soup and a salad," She said to Mike. "And a New York cheesecake with raspberry topping."

"With a dollop of whipped cream," Grace added.

"Enjoy," the girl said, leaving to a duet of thank yous.

They ate in silence. Both picked at their food.

"Grace?" Mike finally said. "You got me telling you my secrets, my sadness. You haven't told me anything about yourself."

"What's to tell? I don't have any secrets, Michael. Well, except this cheesecake is delicious I might have a second piece." She took a bite. "Mmmmm. This is so good I might confess to anything."

"Would you?" Mike asked. They ate and finished, exchanging smiles. Mike struggled with the questions he wanted to ask her, waiting for the right moment. It came when Grace finished her cheesecake, set the fork down, wiped her mouth and sighed, satisfied.

"Hit the spot?"

"The very spot," she replied.

"I'm glad," he added, drinking coffee.

"And your soup?"

"Oh, it was good." He said. "They did it like the French, with toast on top and melted cheese. Almost a meal in itself."

"You're so lucky," Grace said. "You go all over the world for work, don't you?"

"Well," Mike said. "Not all over the world. Believe me, it's mostly work."

"How I envy you. I've not been anywhere...well, Cancun, Mexico at a resort. You must be quite sophisticated."

"Me? Not really," He said, shyly. "I hope I am still the same down-to-earth, uncomplicated baseball player you remember from high school."

"Oh, that reminds me. I forgot to ask you at the reunion, but I have always wondered why you didn't play baseball in college. I thought you were good enough. I used to scan the newspapers. I couldn't find anything."

"I regret not playing in college and I did have some college recruiters ask me to play. But that last game in regionals and the way the season ended devastated me. I needed some time away from the game." Mike took a sip of coffee. "I concentrated on school, worked in the computer lab and I met...Becky."

"You are pretty much the same Michael I remember, with some sadness now." Grace asked, "And me?"

He squinted and pretended a critical eye. "I think the same, yeah." Grace smiled sweetly, with pursed lips. "With a difference," he added.

"Difference? Am I more mysterious?" she joked.

"Yes."

Grace looked surprised. "I was kidding. I'm not mysterious at all."

"You are different," Mike explained. "You have sadness too. I can tell."

She blanched, wiping her mouth the napkin. "I told you I'm a plain and simple suburban housewife."

"All women have secrets, Grace. The difference between women and men is that men consider secrets the mark of good character and that which makes them more important than others. They use secrets like currency. Women, however, have degrees of secrets and have no problem telling or swapping lesser ones. But there are some secrets no woman will ever tell—even to her closest friend."

"Not me," Grace dismissed.

"I know you have...a deep dark secret."

Grace turned and testily said "I told you I have none."

"What if I told you I know what it is and it's something we have in common?"

Grace's eyes narrowed on him across the table.

"You and your sister Chastity share it."

Her eyes grew wide, her mouth tense. "Why are you talking about my sister?" she snapped. "What are you talking about?"

Here was his opportunity. "Grace?" he said, his head cocked sideways, slowly turning the coffee cup. "I want to help. I heard about you and Chastity."

"What?" Her tone verged on anger.

"Someone told me," Mike glanced up at her. "You and your sister were forced into a car and..."

"Told you that?" She spat, throwing her napkin on the table.

"Let me finish..."

"No," Grace said loudly, her hands bunched into fists on the table. "I don't want to hear anymore."

"That you and Chastity were taken to a house and sexually assaulted."

"No!" she cried, waving her hands in front of her face. Tears filled her eyes.

"Grace," he reached across the table for her. She pulled her hand away.

People in the café looked about, startled.

"I want to help," he said firmly. "You never went to the police. Did you? Why?"

"No, I'm not saying anything." Tears streamed down her face.

"I want to know who did that to you and your sister. They should be arrested and punished."

"No...no...I won't tell you anything," she said, grabbing her phone and snatching her bag from the chair. Standing, she said, "Is that why you brought me here? Is this how you get your kicks now?"

"Grace, I want to find them. They need to be punished," he half stood.

"You ought to be ashamed of yourself," she said, and was out the door. Mike saw her dash across the street to her car. Shaken, she dropped her keys trying to open the car door. He slowly sat. Grace got into her car. He could see her shadowy figure inside gripping the steering wheel.

She was right, a cruel trick and he ought to be ashamed. Part of him wanted to know, even if it upset her.

He became aware of people in the café staring. He looked around and they looked away. Glancing back across the street, Grace's car was gone.

"Excuse me?"

Cold coffee in his cup, he sipped. Her reaction told him everything. It was true what Donnie had said. He hated himself for putting her through that.

"Excuse me?" the waitress asked. "Is the lady coming back?"

"No," Mike said, almost under his breath. "She won't be back."

"I'm sorry to hear that," she said. "Would you like more coffee?"

"Yes, I would. Thank you."

Mike sat in the café for the rest of the afternoon, thinking about the lunch with Grace. He would call her and apologize. He might send a tweet or email. He hoped she would forgive his crude tactics. Why did he want to get the truth? Why should he care? This terrible thing that happened to her and her sister was something neither deserved. Whoever did it, got away with it. They got away with a heinous crime, like the men that raped and murdered Becky and had yet to be caught. Or was he feeling guilt? She had dumped him. Perhaps it was the rage and how powerless he felt seeing his wife's defiled body sliced to bloody bits. She suffered. She suffered so much and he wasn't there for her. Could he do something for Grace and Chastity? Could he find the rapists and bring them to justice.

At O'Hare, waiting to board his plane, Mike called. Grace picked up the phone.

"Grace?" he said quickly.

"What do you want?" Her voice cracked.

"I want to apologize..." and the connection went dead.

He called back and got voice mail. "Grace? I want to apologize. I had no right to ask you that. I'm sorry I hurt you." He called later, and got voice mail again. He called over and over and all his calls went to voice mail.

Mike's six hour flight to Manchester provided an opportunity to mull over Grace's reaction at the cafe. He concluded he would find out as much as he could about the rape before he talked to her again. That is, if she ever talked to him again.

Settled in a business class seat, the drone of the turbines lulled him to a half sleep. In a reverie between waking and sleeping, he dreamed of Becky traveling with him to the Rochdale Call Center, in a suburb of Manchester. She didn't travel well and wasn't too keen on English accommodations. The north of England was typically overcast, grey with a chill and damp. Though the rolling hills surrounding the business park where the call center was located looked like the green and pleasant land she had envisioned England to be.

Of course, there was nothing more thrilling than the capital in the late summer with warm early autumn sun. Becky loved walking through Hyde Park or along the Thames estuary as much as the craziness of seeing a band at the Hammersmith Apollo or thrift shopping in Camden Lock.

After Manchester, Mike was scheduled for a trip to Delhi and the India call center in Gurgaon.

Once Becky had accompanied Mike to Delhi. That was one time too many for her. She didn't have the fingers, thumbs or toes to count the ways she hated India. There was the seventeen-hour plane flight for starters. The billion people loudly living lives 24/7. Dire poverty was all around while the fabulously wealthy hid behind walls topped with broken glass. The sun seemed a red hole in a sky smeared by thick brown smoke. That was when it wasn't suddenly raining buckets and flooding streets. The air seemed always filled with the stench of burning tires. The spicy food seared her mouth on the way in and was like fire on the way out—and everything went through her like a Porsche, as the saying goes. Lorry horns all through the night, punctuating the constant swoosh of traffic. Gangs of dirty little children at every intersection swarming like flies around the car, their faces smudging the window, tapping rupees on the glass chanting "lo...lo...lo." The funny expressions Indians would get on their faces when they waggled their heads gesturing a 'yes'. She said it reminded her of bobble heads. And then there was the heat, like an oven. Despite these annoyances, Becky was the perfect visitor, respectful of the elders, chatty and curious about others and on Mike's arm dressed smartly for any company gathering. No one would've guessed that she made Mike swear to never ask her to go back.

Roused from his half-sleep by flight attendants bustling up and down the aisle prepping the plane for landing, Mike remembered Becky was gone forever and his grief, like lead weighed his shoulders down as time and events plodded onward.

Six days later Mike returned from his business trip. He drove back home to West Des Moines, his dark, quiet and empty house. It smelled stale inside. The pictures across the mantle, bookcase and end tables had a fine layer of dust. He emptied his pockets on the table, spilling out wadded pounds, German marks, rupees and coins of the realms. The phone's red light blinked with messages from buddies asking him to play softball in a game three days ago. He hoped Spencer had called. He hadn't. A caller asked for donations for a food drive. Someone running for county supervisor left a robo call political advertisement. It crossed his mind perhaps Grace might've be a called. She would not talk to him. The milk had turned in the refrigerator. Still and stuffy, filled with memories of happier times, the house now made him sad and lonely.

The company gave Mike a week off fully paid after an international trip to recover from jet lag, deal with anything stateside and get his digestive system back on track. Invariably, no matter how careful, he would get Delhi-belly. He was very selective about what he ate, no spicy foods, no street food, no salad and no ice in drinks. But with business lunches with vendors, local managers and supervisors it wasn't easy. Native Indians' digestive systems had the amoebas, parasites and E coli from birth. The company once sent a young business school graduate along with Mike to Delhi. The poor guy lasted one day and became so sick, he soiled himself.

He called Grace. No answer. He left a message.

He got up and walked around the house, restlessly going from room to room, turning lights on in empty rooms, and off. Aimless and lost in his own house, Mike thought about going to the batting cages. He had the urge to hit some balls as hard and as far as he could.

Mike chucked his bat bag into the trunk of his car, slammed the trunk and started for the driver side door. He'd slammed the trunk so hard the lock didn't catch and the lid slowly rose up. "Dammit!" Taking a breath, with both hands, Mike deliberately pushed the lid down and held it. He quickly backed out of the driveway, checked left and right and turned into the street, speeding off.

The radio babbled news talk. Mike impatiently punched through the channels. No, he didn't want music. No, he didn't want sports. No, he didn't want politics. No, he didn't want to hear anything, clicking and off the radio.

There were batting cages in Cleve, north of West Des Moines, not far from Mike's house. Called The Batters Eye USA, or something like that, Mike went a couple of times during softball season and maybe once a month in the off season. Tonight though, tonight he needed to hit some balls.

His fists clenched the steering wheel as he sped past other cars. He spotted a police car ahead and glanced down at the speedometer, letting off the accelerator, tapping the brakes. He was way over the limit.

Staring at the police car in his rear view mirror he was relieved the cop didn't flip on his lights and pull him over.

Lit up like a traveling carnival, The Batters Eye USA featured miniature golf, snack bar inside with video games, go-kart track and outdoor batting cages. Dusk settled in but the semi-circle netted batting cages shown under intense white light. As he grabbed his bat bag from the trunk Mike heard the sounds of batted balls, a comforting sound. Inside the cacophony of noisy kids, beeping arcade games and talking families made for chaos that didn't touch Mike.

For ten dollars you got eight tokens, each token got 20 balls. A high school aged girl with braces on her teeth counted out eight brass tokens on the glass counter and took the ten dollar bill Mike impatiently pushed at her. He raked the tokens off the counter into his hand and thanked the girl with a quick nod.

Walking down the line of cages Mike saw a father crouched on the outside of the batting cage as his young son, wearing an oversized batting helmet, flailed away at each pitched ball.

"Keep your back elbow up!" The father said loudly.

"Eye on the ball!"

"Make contact."

Every pitch from the machine he missed. Frustrated, the boy dropped his arms and looked skyward.

"Elbow," the dad yelled. "Your elbow."

Mike could tell immediately the boy lacked the athletic coordination to hit. His hands started shoulder high then dropped to his waist and he'd end up swinging from the hips. Worse yet, the dad's encouragement sounded more like belittlement. With a little knowledge and confidence he might be okay.

"Come on. You have to make contact."

"I know," the boy whined. "I'm trying."

Mike opened the chain link door to the softball cage at the end. He put the handful of tokens on top of the blue coin box. Unzipping his bat bag he pulled out a 26 ounce Easton Synergy and slipped it back in. He didn't want to swing that bat. He had two other bats in his bag, a Miken Ultra II and Worth Toxic. The Ultra II, a composite bat, was the best softball bat he had ever used. He only swung it in tournaments where it was legal. Batting cage balls would break it in half. Mike pulled out the green Worth Toxic and moved to the center of the batting area. Wind milling his right arm, then his left, Mike tried to loosen up. The Toxic was a heavier composite bat, ASA and U-Trip legal.

He remembered times when Becky came to watch him hit. Sultry summer evenings she stood outside the batting cage with an ice cream cone (vanilla with sprinkles) and between licks say: "nice hit, babe" or "you're pulling your head, honey" or "attaboy". He could almost see her there wearing shorts with her long, slender tanned legs, braless in that beat up, holey old Cubs t-shirt, her hair in a ponytail.

"Eye on the ball!"

"I am!"

Mike took a couple of practice swings then dropped a token into the slot. A red light lit on the pitching machine and a squeaky flywheel started up. Behind the squat machine a conveyor belt moved, dropping softballs into a basket ker-klunk, ker-klunk, ker-klunk. Mike settled himself in the painted batters' box and focused on a ragged cut in the netting, waiting on the machine across an open area of concrete. The ball dropped and the metal arm slowly turned. A dimpled yellow ball arced toward him. With the bat handle loosely held, Mike kept his bat back and waited and waited—then with his head down, stepped and swung. Thwack! The ball loudly came off the bat and sailed into the net at the back of the cage. It was a good, deep, satisfying drive.

He didn't have time to admire it because another pitch came in.

Head. Hips. Hands. Thwack!

Standing in the box, Mike watched the arm pick up another ball and throw. Waiting again until the last moment, he swung and caught the ball on the bottom half. It soared high into the netting overhead.

"Keep your elbow up!"

"If that guy doesn't shut up," Mike muttered, readying for the next pitch. "I'm going to shut him up."

Head. Hips. Hands. Thwack!

Mike tried to get into his batting cage routine. Usually he would start out just hitting away, working on making contact and hitting up the middle. Once he felt confident he had good contact, he would work on placement; hit right, then hit left and hit up the middle. He would know if it was a hit or an out. He could relax then and build up a good sweat. But tonight he couldn't calm down and tried to hit every ball hard, harder and harder than he ever had.

Head. Hips. Hands. Thwack!

He swung quick.

Head. Hips. Hands. Thwack!

He grunted and hit a long fly.

Head. Hips. Hands. Thwack!

He swung and popped it up.

"Dammit," he growled between clenched teeth, dropping another token in the slot.

He gripped the bat tightly now.

Head. Hips. Hands. Thwack!

Foul ball.

Head. Hips. Hands. Thwack!

Line drive.

Each rip made him more and more angry.

A sizzling grounder to the left.

Clang! Mike lined a ball off the pitching machine.

Head. Hips. Hands. Thwack!

Pop up.

Swing and miss.

Head. Hips. Hands. Thwack!

Pop up.

Swing and miss.

"Dammit!"

Swing and miss.

"Dammit! Dammit! Dammit!" Mike flung his bat against the fence and staggered back, falling to a crouch, his head in his hands. His heart pounded in his chest. Tears gushed from his eyes.

"I can't do this, Becks," he whispered. "I can't do this without you. I don't want to go on. I can't."

Pitched balls bounced past him. Then it was quiet, except for Mike's heaving breath.

"You alright, fellah?" a voice outside the cage asked.

Mike looked up from his hands. The boy and his father were standing there.

"Yeah," Mike said, a little embarrassed. "Yeah, I'm fine." He wiped his eyes with the sleeve of his sweat shirt.

"I've just had," he struggled up. "I've had some...bad luck lately." Mike looked at his hands. The skin was torn and bloody.

"You can hit the ball really hard" the boy said.

"Well," Mike said, sniffing back some tears. "Hit the ball and good things can happen."

"We've got to go, Jimmy," the father said, adding. "I hope things work out for you, buddy."

"Thanks," Mike replied, picking up his bat.

"Bye," the boy said.

"Take it easy, all-star," Mike added.

The boy turned back and smiled.

He didn't have the urge to hit any more. Mike slipped his bat into the bag, pocketed the few tokens left and walked out of the cage. Maybe tonight he would sleep.

4

Details, Donnie knew details. He had names. Mike suspected Donnie knew more about Grace's rape than what he told him at the reunion. He called him.

"Yeah, bro," Donnie said. "I'll be here. Sure, tomorrow. Drop by. We'll have a beer. You can buy." He laughed heartily.

Mike drove south on Highway 57 bypassing Park Forest. Donnie lived south of Monee in a trailer park. A farm town, Monee started out as a grange site, grain elevators and railhead. Downtown, as Mike recalled from Sunday drives with his dad, had a gas station going in, a tavern, tap room, feed store, bar, red brick post office and city hall combination, with a gas station on the way out. The town lay beyond the reach of the Metra line so commuter clusters of pressed board, gypsum, Chinese sheet rock. PVC, paint and sod were fewer the farther he went. Mike exited onto Governor's Highway and found himself on two lane black top driving through acre upon acre of green corn, somewhere between knee high and an elephant's eye. The occasional feed lot with cattle or hogs separated soy fields from corn fields.

An entrance to Lincoln's Leisure Acres trailer park came up after a fallow field of discarded farm equipment and scrub brush, just before the gravel pit. Mike turned into the deep rutted gravel road. Bouncing, he drove slow past single and doublewides looking for 15B. Mike spotted a rust-edged singlewide in disrepair. He didn't need to see the tilted mailbox with the faded 15B to know this had to be Donnie's trailer. He pulled in and parked next to a dilapidated burgundy couch on the sunbaked lawn. Stuffed animals and girl's dolls lined the couch cushions. He stepped out, stretched and surveyed the trailer. Wrinkled aluminum foil covered all the windows on the front half. Mike skirted an overturned lawn chair and stepped over beers cans walking to the door.

"Ahhhhh, my man, Shitty Smitty," Donnie shouted, leaning out the screen door. "Welcome to *mi casa.*"

"Hey Donnie," Mike said, picking his way through green garbage bags to the door.

He carefully climbed over the broken wooden stair onto the rotting deck. The screen door squeaked and slammed closed. Mike covered his nose with his hand. The air smelled of cigarettes, fried food, rotted onions and garbage. Worse was the sharp stink of shit from a pair of mucky boots carelessly kicked off on the kitchen floor. Shirts and pants hung where flung on doors and dishes piled precariously in the sink. A halo of flies circulated above the plates, pans and cups.

"Want a beer?" Donnie offered, hunched into the low refrigerator.

"Oh no, not me," Mike said. "Maybe, later."

"Suit yourself," Donnie replied, popping the top of a can of beer and slurping. "Have a seat, man."

Dressed in a dirty t-shirt, grimy jeans and barefoot, Donnie needed a shave, or perhaps he just needed to wash his face.

Mike turned to sit on the couch. He pushed aside a stack of newspapers and uncovered magazine with color pictures of very young and very naked girls. He put a newspaper on the pictures and sat. "So how have you been, Donnie?"

Donnie gazed at Mike with narrow eyes over the top of his beer. He didn't say anything for minute, then slowly tilted the can and took a couple of long swallows.

Donnie's stare made Mike uncomfortable.

"I've been fine," Donnie answered, then pointedly asked, "what the fuck are you doing here?"

"What do you mean?"

"I mean," said Donnie. "I don't hear squat from you in like 30 years...then all of a sudden you wanna be my pal."

"Yeah, I know. I just thought I needed to reconnect with some of my old friends."

"Old friends?" Donnie scoffed, taking a drink. "We were friends?"

"Teammates. I wanted to see how you were doing."

"You gay or something? You come to the wrong place," Donnie said.

"Whoa," Mike protested. "I'm not gay. Like I said, I was wondering how you're doing."

"Really?" Donnie said sarcastically. "You want to know how I'm doing? Shitty...Smitty," he chuckled under his breath. "I've got three ex-wives on my ass for child support. I'm months behind in my lot fees. The best job I can get is at a feed lot slopping hogs. Not to mention my family disowned me. So things are fine, Smitty. Just fucking fine," his voice rose. "You happy now?"

They were silent. Mike sat on the edge of the couch, his hands on his knees, studying Donnie. Traffic sounded loud on the highway outside and a faucet drip drip dripped. Donnie took a pull at his beer and lit a cigarette. No way would Mike leave, not until he got answers. He needed to manipulate Donnie.

"Maybe this wasn't a good idea..." Mike let out a sigh, standing.

"No, man" Donnie said quietly. "I didn't mean to dump on you like that. I just got lots of shit on my mind."

"Sorry to hear that," Mike paused. "What'd you say we go and get a bite to eat?" Adding, "it's my treat."

Donnie sniffed and rubbed his face with his left hand. "Yeah, what the fuck."

"Put on some clean clothes and shoes and you can show me the sights of Monee."

Donnie crushed the empty beer can and flipped it at an overflowing trashcan. He missed and it clattered across the dirty linoleum. "Monee sucks. But I'm hungry and I'll let you buy me dinner." He dropped his cigarette into a coffee cup in the sink. It sizzled. "Let me get my shoes," he said, going into the bedroom. "Hey? We can reminisce about our high school ball team. You should've stuck around for the ceremony at the reunion. Man, we were good team. I don't think Rich High got as close to state for years after."

Mike heard him pissing in the toilet.

"Then how the heck did we lose that game," Mike called after him. "I don't understand how Decker missed line drive hit to his glove side. He had that huge bushel basket first baseman's mitt and he didn't get any leather on it."

"Beats me, man." Donnie replied, zipping up and coming out of the far room. He ducked into a wrinkled t-shirt over his potbelly. "That put the tying run on in the bottom of the ninth." Wearing sliders, he followed Mike down the broken steps. The screen door slammed. "I'll drive," Donnie volunteered. It was a half-hearted offer.

"Oh no," Mike said. "I'll drive. Besides, I'm blocking you. You ride shotgun and tell me the best place to eat." Mike opened the driver's side door.

"Best place to eat is in a little girl's panties." Donnie grinned at his own joke.

Mike got in and picked a black notebook and pair of suede work gloves off the passenger seat as Donnie started to sit.

"What's that?" he asked.

"Oh, just stuff for work," Mike said, flipping the notebook into the back seat and clicking on his seat belt. He put the gloves on the arm rest in front.

"What kind of job you got, man?" Donnie shut the door as Mike turned the ignition. "You go to Pakistan and Africa?"

"No, not really," Mike said with a forced laugh, backing out. "Not Africa or Pakistan. I'm a call center director for a data company in West Des Moines. I go to Asia, England and," Mike paused, smiling. "Rockford."

Donnie chuckled. "How often you have to go to those places?"

Mike put on his turn signal and looked for an opening in crossing traffic. "Every other quarter."

"Quarter? Quarter of what?"

"Twice a year, or when needed." Mike accelerated into a gap in the traffic. Donnie bounced around with the turn. "You may want to put on your seat belt," Mike advised.

"No way," he said. "I ain't getting trapped in this car when you flip it." Donnie relaxed with his elbow out the window. "Don't know how you can do that, man. I could barely stand playing ball with the Beaners."

"So tell me what happened to you after high school," Mike asked. "I heard you signed a minor league contract."

"Yeah, I did, man," Donnie brightened and his voice changed. "I was taken high up in the draft and signed with the Expos."

"You were a damn good right fielder, with a great arm."

"And I could hit," Donnie added. "Damn, I loved to hit."

"Did you ever get to the big club?" Mike turned into downtown Monee.

"Naw, man," he said, looking thoughtfully out the window. "They jacked me around for a bunch of years, riding buses in the Carolina league. I was up and down from instructional to single A, then double A and Triple AAA for a couple games. The only thing that got better was the meal money and seats on the bus. Expo's had Andre Dawson. No way I could crack that right field."

They passed a strip mall with a busy Wal-Mart and modern looking city hall and community center. Downtown Monee surprised Mike, mostly because it had a downtown.

"So where do you want to eat?"

"See that place up there?" Donnie pointed to a grey building with redwood shingles on the front and a small red Old Style neon sign glowing in a narrow black window. "It's Grover's. They know me. They got good food too."

"Okay." Mike said. "Weren't the Cubs interested in you?"

"Cubs, Cards, Houston, I heard all that shit while I'm still riding the bus, playing in the Dominican in the winter. Then I blew out my knee and that was the end of that."

Mike angled into an open spot near the entrance to Grover's and turned off the car.

"That's tough," Mike said, getting out. "How'd it happen?"

"Sprinkler head. A fucking sprinkler head at some fag-ass ball park in Puerto Rico," Donnie laughed hard, doubling over and almost collapsing at the bar entrance. He jerked open the door and stepped into the dark bar. "The funny thing was, man, it was a dirt field. I hooked my foot on a sprinkler head in a fucking dirt ball park." Mike followed Donnie.

"You get outta here!" The bartender yelled, running down to the end of the bar. "You get the hell out of here. I ain't takin' none of your shit tonight."

"Hey, Ricky, man," Donnie pleaded with the hands up. "I'll be cool. I'm here with my buddy. We want something to eat." Ricky didn't have but one tooth in his entire mouth. People along the bar stared indifferently at them.

Mike stood by the door wondering if they were going to be thrown out.

"I'm not taking no crap. I'll have the law here faster than shit. You understand me?"

"Maybe there's another place we can go?" Mike suggested.

"Naw, he's a blow hard," Donnie whispered out of the corner of his mouth. "We're getting a table, Ricky. Just lighten up, man."

Mike trailed Donnie to a small table in the back. Country music played low. A TV flickered, mounted to the ceiling at the end of the bar.

An overweight, middle-aged woman with greasy blonde hair came over.

"Hey, good looking—what's cooking?"

"Shut up, Donnie. You need menus?" she asked.

"I do," Mike said, sitting. He took the proffered laminate sheet from the woman.

"I don't," Donnie said. "Two beers and a cheeseburger for me."

"Mike looked up and down the menu. "Can I get a bacon cheeseburger?" he asked, handing back the menu.

"Sure can."

"Thank you," Mike said.

"Thanks, beautiful," Donnie added.

"You're welcome," she replied to Mike. "And fuck you, Donnie.

He chuckled.

"What about you, man," Donnie said, leaning forward. "You were a fucking stud third base. I remember that regional game and you went flat out vertical for a hard one hop ground ball up the line. I think you threw to first from your knees. That play almost won the game."

Mike nodded and smiled. "Yeah, I had pretty good reflexes back then."

"If we won that it was the state championships," Donnie said wistfully. The beers came. Donnie drank.

"We didn't hit," Mike offered. He recalled Donnie dropping a routine fly ball in right and letting another base runner on.

"Shit we didn't," Donnie agreed, slamming his beer down on the table. "I got a triple and a double and you chipped in with a couple of singles and a double. Even Gary Watson got a hit. It was Decker, that fuck. He didn't hit shit. I died on third base as he hit a weak ass grounder for a double play. Then in the tenth we had the go ahead run on second and he takes strike three on a hit and run call."

"That was me," Mike said. "I was out by about six feet on the throw from the catcher to third."

"Decker," Donnie snarled. "That guy stunk. The only reason he was on the team was old man Decker was a big shot in the school administration."

"I thought you were pals with Decker? Didn't he give you a job after baseball was over?"

"Yeah, for his real estate company. A shit job."

"You were pals with Watson too, our shortstop."

"We were buds since Blackhawk Elementary, man."

"You still friends?"

"He's a wuss," Donnie said. "A monkey suit guy in a bank in Homewood. Got himself a new young wife and kids in Flossmoor—fuck Flossmoor."

Mike made a mental note; Gary worked at a bank in Homewood and lived in Flossmoor. Donnie and Gary were inseparable in grade school and into high school. But something had happened between them and it showed the day of the game. No one knew why. Mike recalled that Decker was involved, though he didn't know how.

"Since you're buying," Donnie spoke up. "Can I get a shot of Everclear?"

"Of what?" Mike asked.

"Ever...Everclear. You ain't never heard of Everclear?" Donnie sounded amazed.

"No, I never have," Mike admitted. "But if you want one, it's on me."

"'Ready for another beer?"

Mike, who had been sipping his first beer, was about to say no, but Donnie had two fingers up, whistling at the bar.

"Two beers'n two Everclear," he shouted.

Ricky, leaning behind the bar working a toothpick around his tooth, looked disgusted and skeptical. "And who's paying for this?"

Mike waved.

"Who's that, Donnie?" Ricky asked, spitting something into the sink. "Your parole officer?"

"Shut up, Ricky." Donnie rose menacingly from his chair, then slowly sunk back down.

Drinks arrived before the food and Mike thought to himself that he had to be careful with the booze he was pushing on Donnie. He wanted him drunk and talkative, not drunk and passed out. Donnie was anything but cautious, tossing the shot glass of Everclear down his throat and chasing it with a long pull at his beer. He shook his head, yelped with pleasure and exclaimed, "Yeah, that's more like it."

Mike saw that the harder liquor was starting to affect Donnie. His eyes drooped, blinked and looked unfocused. He sat with both elbows on the round table, his beer firmly clutched in his left hand, a cigarette in the right.

"You ain't keeping up, Smitty," Donnie laughed, pointing to the Everclear and beer in front of Mike.

"You're right," Mike said, taking the shot glass to his lips. He flipped his head back as if slugging the shot back, but he kept the glass upright and his lips shut tight. The clear liquor sloshed a bit and burned his lips. Mike could tell Everclear was an extremely potent drink. "Wow!" He said. "Wow! That's some powerful stuff."

Donnie's guttural laugh came from deep in his throat. "It's the best, man. I'd like me another..." He paused, asking, "If that's cool with you?"

"Hey, I said my treat. You couldn't chug another," Mike challenged.

"Watch me."

"Take this one," Mike slid the shot glass across the table.

"That's yours, man. I'm not taking yours."

"I'll get another," Mike assured him. He got the attention of Ricky behind the bar, holding up two fingers.

"Beers?" Ricky asked warily.

"One Everclear, one beer," Mike called back.

Ricky looked at him a long moment, then said, "You got it."

The burger baskets and booze reached the table simultaneously.

"This looks good," Mike said to the waitress, then whispered to her. "Can I get an O'Doul's, or something like that?"

Donnie looked from the shot of Everclear to the burger and chose the shot, tilting his head back and drinking it in one gulp. "Damn! That's good."

Mike, the burger in both hands, chewing, agreed. "These are damn good burgers." He watched silently as Donnie tried to squirt ketchup on his French fries, missing the basket and putting a red puddle on the table. Mike studied Donnie. He was drunk, though not drunk enough.

"So, Donnie," Mike said. "You said at the reunion you've been married a couple of times?"

"Shit yeah," he spat, biting into a cluster of French fries. "Four fuckin' bitches."

"Thought you said three? They gave you a hard time?"

"Yeah three, whatever," Donnie laughed and bits of chewed fries splattered the table. "Naw, I gave them a hard time...with my big cock, right up the ass!"

Those nearby frowned at Donnie's language. Mike cleared his throat and tried to sound calm. "They didn't like that?"

"Who cares what they liked," Donnie was getting louder and could be heard even though the bar was noisy.

"All bitches like it up the ass. If they say no, I make'em like it." He was getting boisterous. He tried to pick up his burger, but it slipped from his hands back into the basket.

"Did you drink my Everclear?" Mike motioned to the empty shot glass.

"Huh?" Donnie was confused. "I thought you drank it?"

"I didn't. I'll get another. Drink your beer," Mike urged him. Donnie slowly drank, slopping beer down his shirt.

"Fuck," Donnie breathed. "We're drinking a lot pretty damn fast. You drink this much all the time?"

"All the time," Mike said, motioning with his beer as if he was about to take a drink. "And you got kids, right Donnie?"

"Kids? Yeah, I got kids. I'll tell you about kids," he pointed a limp fry at Mike and fixed him with narrow eyes. "Ungrateful little bastards. Gimme gimme gimme. Not even sure they were mine. Gimme gimme. Sit around watching TV, playing video games, all day. Fat fuckin' mother don't do shit...shit!"

Mike had enough of his cheeseburger, putting it in the basket and wiping his hands with a paper napkin. Donnie mumbled, but not to Mike. He was slumped low, his head down and wagging. Drunk, and almost drunk enough for Mike.

"...fat, mouthy...always bitchin' at me to get a job...get a job. Shut up, bitch...I'm a fuckin' ballplayer. I got a minor league contract. I'm gonna get disability for my knee..." A long line of drool dripped from his slack lower lip.

"My second wife," Donnie started. "When I got home she'd make me drop my pants and smell my dick." He laughed and guzzled beer. "Everything was cool until the night I came home and she smelled her sister's pussy on my dick."

"You got another Everclear coming. How about some tequila?" Mike suggested. "That would put a nice buzz on the evening."

"Tequila?" Donnie raised his head and blinked trying to focus. "You're an animal, man. Shitty Smitty. Decker gave you that name. Decker, Decker and his pervert dad.

Those guys," he snarled. "The old man's a big shit state politician now. Fuckin' untouchable."

The waitress came up with the shot of Everclear and Mike's O'Douls. She cleared away the empty glasses that surrounded Donnie and his uneaten burger. "Is he alright?" she looked sideways at Donnie, sounding worried.

Donnie continued talking. "My first wife was some Puerto Rican bitch. I think we had a kid, not sure we got a divorce."

"He's fine," Mike assured her. "We're old pals celebrating. I think we're done with the food. Can I get a couple shots of tequila?"

"Top shelf?"

"No," Mike replied firmly, with his finger upraised. "I want two shots of the worse and cheapest tequila you got." He enjoyed saying that.

"Okay," she said slowly. "He's not driving, is he?"

"I'll drive you, baby," Donnie said, bleary-eyed and smiling. "You just bend over."

Whatever concern she had expressed for Donnie a moment before vanished with his crude comment. "Put a sock in it, Donnie," she shot back. "I'll be back with your tequila."

"And the check, please," Mike called after her.

"You got it."

"Whud ya say we grab that bitch and take her out back and screw her crazy?" His laugh was throaty and nasty. He fumbled for a cigarette.

"Like Decker and his dad?" Mike said, fishing for a response.

"Decker and his dad?" Donnie said through clenched teeth. "She's too old for them. How the hell you know about that?"

"Everybody knows about them," Mike calmly replied. There was something behind Donnie's hatred of their high school first baseman, and his father.

"They're evil, man."

"Yeah, evil, Donnie. Fucking evil." Mike played along.

The waitress came up with the shots of tequila and check.

"Drink up, man," Mike said, leaning over and slapping Donnie on the shoulder. "Maybe we can go see ol' Decker and his dad." Mike held the bill sideways to catch some light in the dimly lit bar. Two burgers $18, beer, shots $75, Mike read with no surprise. He reached into his back pocket and pulled out his wallet. Donnie had drunk half the tequila and a gulp of Everclear with his eyes fixed on Mike's wallet. Mike fingered six $20 bills and pulled them out.

"Damn, Smitty," Donnie exclaimed. "You got a shit wad of money there. What happened? You get a lot of money when you killed your wife?"

The waitress' eyes went from Donnie to Mike, and the money he held up to her.

"He's joking," Mike said.

"I'll be back with your change," She said, turning.

Donnie's comment angered Mike, but he kept a straight face. "I don't need any change," he called to the waitress.

"Thank you."

"Lend me some money, Smitty."

"You want to borrow some money?" Mike asked, putting his wallet back into his pocket. "Drink your tequila first."

Donnie drank slowly, unable to chug the tequila like he had the Everclear, and shivered. "Whoa. That was a shot. This ain't the best. They screwed you, man. Yeah, C'mon, Smitty, lend me ten thousand bucks."

"I don't have that much," Mike feigned being apologetic.

"How about a hundred?" Donnie asked.

"A hundred?" Mike pretended to think it over. "Tell ya what," he added. "I'll drive and we can go over to see Decker and his dad. Now don't let that last shot of Everclear go to waste. When we see Decker I'll loan you the hundred. Deal?"

"Shit," Donnie could barely talk. "I thought you were gay, getting me drunk so you can fuck me? Oh, you want to go to Decker's for one of his parties, huh?" He paused, losing his train of thought. "Give me two hundred."

"No," Mike chuckled. "I only got a hundred on me. He pushed the last shot over to Donnie. His grip was slack, so Mike made sure he got the small glass to his mouth. "Chug-a-lug."

"For a hundred," Donnie sputtered out, swallowing. He shivered again, longer this time.

"Attaboy, Donnie."

Swaying in his chair, Donnie held up the empty shot glass triumphantly, pleased with his accomplishment.

Mike knew he had him now. Donnie had drunk too much too quickly and was on the verge of passing out. He'd soon be getting sick, mixing beer, hard liquor and greasy hamburger. "Hey! Hey, Donnie," Mike called. Donnie had fallen back in this chair with his chin on his chest. "Wake up, man," Mike shook his shoulder. "We're going to Decker's for the party, right?"

"Huh?" Donnie's head bobbed up. "Wah?"

"Stand up," Mike's tone was loud, firm. "Stand up. We're getting out of here?"

"Oh, man," Donnie complained. "Let's just hang out here for a little while."

"No way," Mike said. "We're going to Decker's, man." Mike grabbed Donnie by the back of his neck and under his shoulder, jerking him upright. Staggering, scrabbling, Donnie got his legs under himself.

"You like that scared teen pussy too? Ow, man, easy," Donnie whined.

"Oh yeah, you know I do. The younger the better."

"Seven's heaven and eight's too late," Donnie snorted, lurching forward.

Mike shoved and pushed, manhandled and maneuvered Donnie through the bar to the door.

"Thanks for taking the garbage out," Ricky hissed. "Come again, anytime."

"Sha'up, Ricky," Donnie mouthed. "I'll kig your ass."

People in the bar laughed.

Mike got Donnie through the door and outside to the car. Night had descended on downtown Monee. Neon and street lights shined off Mike's car as he laid Donnie across the hood while he unlocked the doors. "Where's my hundred? Did you forget my hundred?" Donnie mumbled.

"Got it right here," Mike said. "I'll give it to you when we get to Decker's party." He jerked Donnie roughly up from the hood and pushed him around to the side, and opened the back door.

"Decker's party? Fuck, Smitty," Donnie was saying. "I'll suck your cock for a hundred. Gimme your cock." He reached out as Mike shoved him into the back seat.

"Shut the hell up, Donnie." His feet hung out and Mike noticed he'd lost a slider. He pushed his legs into the back and slammed the door.

"You awake back there?" Mike shouted, getting behind the steering wheel. There was a grunt. Mike turned and slapped Donnie hard across the face. "Don't you pass out on me you asshole!"

The slap and shout startled Donnie awake. "Wha? Wha?" he mumbled his mouth slack. A line of spit dangled off his lip.

"We're going to Decker's party, with all the young girls." Mike's open hand again went hard across the side of Donnie's face. Donnie tried to fend off the blow, but it was after Mike had slapped him. "You're going to tell me all about Decker's party. And you're going to tell me about Grace House and her sister Chastity. You remember Grace and Chastity? Remember?"

Donnie was confused. "Gr-Grace? From school?"

Mike started up the car and backed out.

"Yes! Grace. You told me she was raped. Was she raped at Decker's party?" Mike yelled over the seatback.

"I...I don't know what you're saying." Donnie sounded scared. "Let me out. Let me out of the car."

Mike sped up and clicked the locks from the drivers' side door panel.

"I don't know what happened to her and her sister. That's high school. They were just walking in the shopping center, coming back from the Aqua Center. We were driving around and Decker's dad sees them. Decker had a knife and made her and her sister get in the car. Somebody stabbed her. Then...then, we went to a house," he trailed off.

Mike turned into Donnie's trailer park.

"This ain't Decker's. I don't know shit," Donnie wailed. "He told her he would kill her parents if they talked. I don't know nothin', man."

"Yeah you do you piece of shit." Mike pulled in behind Donnie's rusted out car. "Who else was there?" He shut off the car and tugged on a pair of suede work gloves. He opened the door locks and got out. "I am going to get the truth out of you if I have to beat it out of you. You will pay...all of you will pay for what you did to Grace and Chastity."

Mike jerked open the back door and dragged Donnie out. He struggled, flailing his arms to defend himself and trying to kick Mike.

"You will tell me the truth, you son of a bitch." Mike held Donnie up against the side of the car.

"They fucked her....we all fucked her. You did too," Donnie was saying as if begging for his life.

"No, I didn't!"

"You're a liar."

Mike lost it. He swung short and quick into Donnie's jaw. Donnie's head snapped back, banging into the roof of the car.

"I'll kill you, you shit," Donnie said as he fell sideways.

Mike had Donnie's T-shirt bunched in his left hand and punched his right fist into Donnie's gut. He doubled over, gagged and fell to his knees on the gravel drive.

"You will tell me who was there. Who raped Grace and Chastity?"

"Fuck...fuck...she was being fucked by other guys and yelling leave my sister alone, leave my sister alone. She's innocent, leave her alone."

"Who yelled? Who?" Mike hauled Donnie up and pushed him against the car.

"Grace yelled leave my sister alone. They made her suck dick, suck everybody's dick."

Mike's fist slammed into Donnie's face. Blood gushed out his nostrils and dribbled down his chin. Dazed, Donnie sank to all fours. Mike stood and noticed his notebook on the gravel next to Donnie. It must've come out when he dragged Donnie from the back. Blood puddled on the notebook's hard cover.

"What else?" Mike demanded, calmer and quieter.

"I don't know what else, ask Gary." Donnie moaned. "You broke my nose, you fuck." The blood on Donnie's face glistened in the street light. "She's a fuckin' whore."

Mike's kick caught Donnie squarely in the face. Something sparkled flying out of his mouth with spit and blood. "Who said she was a whore?" Donnie rolled to his side.

No answer.

"Who said she was a whore? Decker?"

No answer.

Donnie was out cold.

Mike, breathing hard, stared down at Donnie. He was covered in blood, his breath raspy and shallow. A spreading wet stain ran down Donnie's pants. Pieces of the story fit together now. That poor girl, Mike thought. Grace and her sister raped and keeping the secret inside for all these years. Decker and his dad held parties with underage girls. Gary was involved. Gary didn't seem the type. Decker's dad was a bigwig in the state government. You never know about people.

Taking out his wallet, Mike counted out five $20 bills. He wiped blood and snot from Donnie's face on the bills and stuffed them down the front of Donnie's shirt. He tossed the bloodstained notebook and suede gloves into the backseat. He should've felt satisfied, yet all he felt was disgust. His spit landed on Donnie's face.

Slowly Mike backed out of the gravel drive. He'd head back to Park Forest and get a room for the night. Tomorrow he'd find the bank in Homewood where Gary worked and they would have a talk.

5

GPS directed Mike to a Country Hotel in Matteson. Workng the late shift, a young Indian man with dark features came out from a backroom to the counter. Mike could smell the saffron and cayenne cooking in a backroom.

"Hello" he said. "I don't have a reservation but was wondering if you have a room available for the night?"

"Certainly," the Indian said, waggling his head side to side. "Smoking or non-smoking?" He had a thick accent and curry on his breath.

"Great, non-smoking please," Mike said. The accent wasn't refined, more rural and southern than northern Brahmin to his ear.

"I will need a major credit card," he said in the sing-song fashion some Indians speak. "Just for the one night, then?"

"Yes," Mike replied, reaching into his back pocket for his wallet.

"And please..." the Indian man asked, "Fill in this form?"

"Okay." Mike handed him his credit card.

"Oh gracious," the Indian exclaimed, taking Mike's credit card. "Are you well, sir?"

"Pardon?"

The Indian pointed to Mike's right arm. In the bright light of the lobby Mike saw the sleeve of his tan sports jacket stained with blood up to the elbow, Donnie's blood.

"I, ah, cut myself earlier tonight," Mike stammered, while filling out the form.

"Do you require medical assistance?" the Indian asked.

"No, no, I'm fine."

"May I see your driver's license?" There was a suspicious tone to the Indian's voice.

"Sure. Is there a problem?"

"None, sir."

Mike slipped his driver's license out of his wallet and pushed it across. The Indian took the credit card and driver's license and busied himself under the counter. Mike completed the form and turned it around. It crossed his mind to ask where the Indian was from, but since the man had noticed the blood on his sleeve he decided not to be so friendly.

After an uncomfortable few minutes, the Indian handed Mike his credit card and license. While Mike put them back in his wallet, the Indian slapped on the counter a paper holder with two plastic swipe cards inside. He leaned across.

"Your room is number 275, sir," he said. "Here are your room cards. We are here," he added, pointing to a red star on a frayed map taped to the counter. "Your room is..." he searched a moment. "Ah, it is at the end of the second floor." He stood up and smiled very yellow teeth. "We have a continental breakfast served from 6:30 to 10AM."

"Thank you," Mike said, backing away from the counter. "Is there another door that I can use?" He motioned toward the far end of the hotel.

"Oh certainly, sir, yes," the Indian said, again waggling his head. "And take care of yourself."

Mike waved on the way out the door. After driving to the side entrance, he got out and took his overnight bag and laptop from the trunk. He noticed a green dumpster in a dark corner of the parking lot. It occurred to Mike to get rid of his bloody sports jacket. What if Donnie called the police and they tracked him to this hotel? Mike took off his sports jacket, tossed it into the trunk and slammed it shut. He'd have to hold on to it for now.

In the room, Mike snapped on the overhead light, put his bag in the chair and slipped his laptop off his shoulder, placing it on the round table. He sat on the edge of the bed suddenly feeling exhausted. He fell back with his arms outstretched.

"What am I doing?" he wondered aloud. For a long time he lay there, staring at the white popcorn ceiling. He had no answer. It was started, "and I'm going to finish it," he whispered, sitting up.

There were five work related messages on his phone, but nothing from Grace. Two of the calls were from the India call center. The time difference was 12 hours ahead, so it would be early morning of the next day there.

"Vineet? This is Mr. Smith. Sorry I didn't get your call earlier." He listened a moment. "That's right. We have cleared the two new hires. You should have the paper work to you by your tomorrow. Did you get the UPS issue sorted out?" Mike listened. "We need an uninterrupted power source for the servers. That has to be done this morning. Get Mr. Sharma to find someone." Mike listened again. "Good. Good. I will talk to you next week in our conference call. Very good. Good-bye."

Two other calls were voice mails, one from the supervisor in the Manchester Call Center about needing headsets and the other from the manager of the Rockford center inviting him to lunch at the end of the week. There was a missed call. Though no voice mail. Mike checked the number. It was an Illinois area code, but not Grace's number. The call had come in only a half hour ago. Tired, and ready to sleep, Mike put the charger cord on his phone and set it on the table. He had the bloody notebook and put it on the bedside table.

Lying in bed, Mike turned on the television and opened the notebook. He had notes from his conversation with Donnie at the reunion when he first learned of the rape of Grace and Chastity. He leafed past these pages, and pages of his lunch conversation with Grace at the café. He had pages and pages with single notations: "Called Grace to apologize. VM." Mike opened to an empty page and wrote: "Went to Monee and saw Donnie Inge..." In an abbreviated form, he wrote out the evening's activity with Donnie. He ended succinctly writing, "I punched the fucker and he went unconscious."

Exhausted, Mike switched off the TV and closed his eyes, just to rest them.

Mike shuffled his feet. The black dress shoes, buffed to a high sheen, pinched his toes and squeezed his heels. The wing tip collar and bow tie on his starched white shirt chaffed his neck. The grey tuxedo jacket, while long in the sleeve, was tight across his shoulders. Mike sweat under the hot lights. The red cheeked, cherub faced Pastor, swayed before him in long robes, cradling his bible in both hands. He gave Mike a questioning look, as if he thought Mike about to faint. "Are you alright, son?"

"Fine, father," Mike whispered.

Mark Larch from Pennsylvania, Mike's college buddy and best man, hummed an Elvis tune, oblivious to the pastor, lights and the people filing into the church and sitting at the pews. Mark's wedding day eve night out had turned quite exciting. Tiffany, Becky's maid of honor, unsteady on wobbling heels, clutched a bouquet in her trembling hands. Makeup couldn't conceal the dark circles under her eyes and greenish pallor to her cheeks. It clashed with her lavender dress. Tiff and Mark traded glances and nearly burst out laughing. Serves me right, Mike thought, leaving early from dinner and never thinking those two needed a chaperone.

St. Peter's Lutheran, in Schaumburg was decorated with banks of flowers. Pews in the narrow 19th century chapel filled with wedding guests. On the bride's side, Mrs. Devereux sat bolt upright, first row front. Dressed in a fashionable dark print dress, hat and veil, she wore a stern expression as if not totally approving. Becky's brother and sister-in-law bounced babies on their laps, next to her. The rest of the Devereux and Spencer clan filled pews eight rows back. Mike glanced over to the groom's side of the chapel and exchanged a smile and wink with his mother. She and Mike's dad, his uncle and wife, another uncle and his boyfriend and a few nieces and nephews were scattered across three rows of pews. Mike's father wore his best brown suit while his mother had dressed in a simple beige dress, with white gloves. She couldn't raise her chin off her chest in the presence of the well off, well-dressed and imperious Mrs. Devereux.

"We're caught in a trap," Mark sang. "Can't get out..."

"Knock it off," Mike hissed.

"Sorry, bro. Tiff? Tiff? Where're we going after the reception?"

Tiffany giggled, waved him off, then bent forward and coughed, looking like she was about to throw up.

The church pipe organ struck the opening notes of the Wedding March.

People rose.

Mike turned. At the top of the aisle the double doors opened and morning sunlight streamed in. Becky in a long white gown stepped into the light. Speechless, Mike caught sight of her. Her Uncle Wiggly accompanied her. The family called him Uncle Wiggly because of his pigeon toed gait and round hips that sashayed side to side as he walked. Stout and silver at the temples, dressed in a grey tuxedo that matched Mike's, he escorted his niece Becky arm in arm and down the aisle.

The white silk wedding gown, with its drop waist billowing into a wide skirt and train, accentuated Becky's tall, slim figure. The bodice and sleeves were embroidered Chantilly Lace matching her veil. A single strand of family heirloom pearls and a bouquet of white roses completed her ensemble. Uncle Wiggly twisted and turned looking back, worrying about stepping on the dress' long train. As she glided down the aisle all the women breathed "oh" and brought out their handkerchiefs. Mike's mother watched her in awe. Then she mouthed to Mike's dad "she's lovely." Becky did look like an angel and Mike wanted to run to her, sweep her off her feet and twirl her round and round.

Uncle Wiggly handed off Becky and shuffled to the side.

"You look gorgeous."

"Batter up, slugger," she replied.

The Wedding March ended.

Tiffany burped and put her hand over her mouth. Becky glowered at her. Through the veil Mike could see her eyes wide open. He shrugged. Becky saw Mark grinning at her.

"If she hurls I'm going to kick his butt."

Loudly, Mrs. Devereux cleared her throat, startling the pastor who seemed to be daydreaming. He opened his bible.

"Dearly beloved we are gathered here together..."

The ceremony and reception went off without Tiffany vomiting and Mark dropping the ring. During the reception, Mike and Becky, their heads together, snickered about Mark and Tiffany's sudden romance, then realized the two had disappeared.

Newly wed, Mike and Becky drove up Lake Shore Drive and checked into the Drake Hotel as dusk settled and the Chicago skyline came to light. The venerable Gold Coast hotel, with its old world style and opulent décor would be their honeymoon hideaway until Monday when Mike went back to his job and Becky attended graduate classes at the University of Chicago. Their fifth floor suite overlooked Oak Street Beach and Lake Michigan beyond. Finally alone, they drank champagne in the Drake's swanky Coq D'or, spiriting away a bottle of Perrier-Jouet to their suite.

The big, bright moon hung full in the dark night sky over Lake Michigan, shimmering across the water. A shaft of silver light streamed into the suite from windows facing the lake. Becky reclined naked on the chaise, her lithe body in shadow and light. Her eyes glistened gazing upward at Mike. Slowly, she tilted her champagne glass and poured the wine down her chest. It rolled to her belly and left bubbles in her black triangle. Plop. A drop fell to the carpet. Mike went down to a knee and leaned forward between Becky's open thighs. "Oh, Mikey," she whispered.

He woke with a start, blinking at the morning light flooding the motel room.

"No...no...," Mike repeated. "I want to go back...please." He closed his eyes, falling asleep again.

"Oh, Mikey." He heard her say.

He looked up. Her head seemed cocked at an odd angle. Her hair looked messed and matted with dry leaves and twigs sticking out. Reaching up, Mike touched her blue face. Her head slipped off her shoulders and bumped to the chaise.

"It's okay, Becks. I have it." He picked up her head and put it back on her shoulders. It wouldn't stay.

Her leg dropped to the floor. Quickly, Mike picked the leg from the floor. It fell to pieces in his hands like hunks of meat. Frantic now, he scrambled to put her back together.

"Becks...no...please, God," he yelled.

Light burst into his eyes. His lungs ached. He couldn't breathe. He hugged the pillow, a pillow wet from tears and sweat. Mike rolled onto his back staring at the ceiling of the motel room. He curled up and cried.

Pulling himself together, shaving, showering, Mike then went down to the breakfast nook. He took a corner table and opened up his laptop. While Windows loaded, he went for a cup of coffee, orange juice and blueberry muffin from the breakfast array on the counter. He logged onto the hotel's Wi Fi and checked his emails. His work account just had CC emails from his assistant and HR regarding the new hire's paper work to the India center; and a company-wide announcement about a quarterly town hall meeting. A softball buddy had sent jpegs of bikini girls in his personal gmail account. With work related issues cleared, Mike went on Google and keyed in Banks Homewood, Illinois. He sipped coffee from the Styrofoam cup and munched the muffin while scrolling through the results. There were nine banks, with branches in Homewood. Mike set his coffee to the side, brushed crumbs off his fingers and clicked on the first bank web page. He scanned the home page and found a link to executives. He scrolled down the page looking for Gary Watson. No luck on the first bank. He clicked the back button to return to his search results.

He clicked on a second bank, the Bank of Lake Michigan, with locations in Illinois, Indiana, Michigan and Wisconsin. Mike opened the Illinois branches and clicked on the Homewood branch. He wondered if Donnie really knew what he was talking about.

The Homewood branch of the bank had its own page and a second page of executives. Mike noticed at the bottom of the page was a banner ad for Decker Real Estate. Scrolling down, he spotted Gary.

"Gotcha," Mike breathed, taking a sip of coffee.

Branch manager of the Bank of Lake Michigan, Gary Watson, resplendent in a blue suit, red tie and American flag lapel pin, grinned from the internet page. On the heavy side, with a reddish fleshy face and thinning hair, the years had put weight on the Rich High Rockets wiry and agile shortstop.

Mike back tracked to the Homewood branch page and opened the Contact Us link for a phone number and address. He jotted down the address and cross street in his notebook. He tapped in the phone number on his phone and pressed the phone symbol. He went back to the executive page to see if Gary had a direct line while the phone rang. He didn't.

"You have reached the Bank of Lake Michigan, Homewood branch. For English press 1." Mike pressed the 1 key. "Our hours of operation are 10AM to 4PM Monday through Friday. If you know the party you wish to reach please input the first three letters of their last name. Or stay on the line to leave a message in our general mailbox."

Mike tapped W...A...T on the keypad. There was a series of rings.

"You have reached Gary Watson, manager of the Bank of Lake Michigan Homewood. I am currently out of the office. Please leave a message and I will promptly return your call. Have a blessed day." The line beeped.

"Blessed day?" Mike thought.

"Hey, Gary," he said, his voice unsteady at first. "It's Mike Smith, third base, Rich High Rockets, remember? How have you been, buddy? I'm passing through Homewood and wanted to stop by and say hello." Mike paused. "I have some business I want to talk to you about. I'll drop by this afternoon. We can catch up. Take care." He clicked off and sat back in his chair venting a sigh, then got up and refilled his coffee cup from the carafe. There, he thought, from Donnie to Gary; from Gary to who? Decker?

Traffic on highway 30 east was sporadic driving into Chicago Heights, with some congestion through the city. Mike made reasonable time when he turned north onto Dixie Highway.

He spotted a green dumpster in a strip mall parking lot and pulled alongside. He popped the trunk. Donnie's blood on the sleeve had dried stiff and brown. Hurriedly, Mike turned out all the pockets of the jacket inside out making sure there were no receipts or other traceable items. He wadded the sports jacket into a bunch and dropped it in the dumpster. He felt tight with fear and did his utmost to not look around nor appear suspicious. He tossed the bloody gloves in the dumpster and moved some bags of garbage over the jacket and gloves. He closed the trunk and drove slowly out of the parking lot, merging back into the traffic on the Dixie Highway.

As he drove, he keyed in Grace's number. It rang and rang and rang until it went to voice mail. "Grace, it's Mike again. I need to talk to you. Please call me back." He dropped his phone on the seat. He had to keep trying to reach her.

Once out of Chicago Heights the surrounding area changed dramatically. There were clusters of upscale subdivisions, each cluster becoming more and more affluent. Golf courses, country clubs and trendy shopping malls lined the highway. Mike bet himself he wouldn't see a White Castle all the way to Homewood.

Home Sweet Homewood declared the sign as Mike entered the city limits. He checked the dashboard clock—it was 10:05 AM. The bank should have just opened.

Dixie Highway became Chicago Road as he slowly drove toward Homewood center.

The downtown was dotted with quaint Victorian-era storefronts, with interlocking red brick paver's sidewalks and ornate pseudo-gaslight style street lamps. The trees were squat and well-trimmed, between brick benches. It was all too perfect, the mock old century style.

The Bank of Lake Michigan was on the corner of Harwood and Ridge streets. Mike turned left and immediately located it. At the corner was the Metra and Amtrak station. Across the train tracks was the wide green grassy expanse of the Ravisoe Country Club. He parked in the middle of the block, within sight of the entrance. He was in front of a kosher teriyaki chicken restaurant, between a beauty salon and bridal shop. Kosher teriyaki? It made sense for the suburbs when Mike thought about it.

He took his black notebook from the passenger seat and got out. The town center was quiet, with few pedestrians, in the mid-morning sun. A Metra train beeped and rattled in the distance, coming into the station. Mike pumped three quarters into the parking meter—20 minutes per quarter. He didn't think he would be talking to Gary for a full hour. The teriyaki restaurant was dark, closed until 4PM. A young woman, accompanied by an older woman who, judging by the similarity of features, had to be her mother, were bickering back and forth, entering the bridal shop. A car waited for Mike to cross the sidewalk at the bank's ATM drive through. The bank front was all glass and beige stucco with a heavy double door in the middle.

Young tellers worked at windows in the semi-circular rotunda, helping people who were queued in the middle. It was all marble and glass echoing conversations and footballs.

"I can help the next person," a girl called out and it reverberated slightly.

A bony woman with dirty blonde hair at a desk to Mike's left, chatted on the phone. Behind her were glass offices with desks and computers. Mike looked down the row of offices to the largest on the end. There was a large man in a grey suit standing with his back to the window. He was on the phone and gesturing in a very animated conversation.

"May I help you?" the blonde asked Mike, replacing the phone in its cradle.

"Yes, you certainly may," Mike said with a smile. "I'm here to see Gary Watson."

"Do you have an appointment?"

"Ah yes," Mike said. "I called ol' Gar this morning and said I would be in to see him. We're old friends."

"I'll see if he's available," she said, picking up the phone. "And your name?"

"It's Smith, Mike Smith."

"It's a good thing you came in this morning," the woman said after pressing keys on the pad. "Mr. Watson said he had to be leaving early today."

"Oh...that is a good thing," Mike quietly agreed.

He looked at Gary's office. He was off the phone and at his desk. He picked up the phone.

"Mr. Watson? There's a Mike Smith here to see you."

Gary's head swung quickly around to the front. His expression was not one of joy to see his old school chum. He saw Mike, then broke into a wan smile and weakly waved Mike to come over.

"He'll see you now," she said, smiling.

"Thank you," Mike curtly replied, crossing the beige marble rotunda to Gary's office.

At the door to his office, Gary held out his hand. "Smitty," he said a little too friendly.

"Gary," Mike responded. "Or should I call you Shorty." They shook hands and Gary motioned Mike to a chair in front of his desk.

"Ha! Good one. I have not been called that in quite some time," he said, sitting behind his desk.

"Who gave you that name?" Mike asked, settling into the chair.

Gary sighed, leaning back in his black leather chair. "Decker did." He rolled his eyes upward.

"You're really not short," Mike said.

"Shade over 5 foot 10," Gary replied. "Decker would laugh and say it wasn't because of my height."

Mike snorted, and shook his head. Gary was larger than he remembered, doughy and filling out his grey suit, blue tie and vest. His face was rosy, round and fleshy. Gary's hairline was retreating from his wide forehead, except for some hairs like a boat's prow plowing down the middle of his head.

"That's way better than the name he gave you," Gary said, fidgeting with a pen between his fingers and rocking in his chair.

"Yup," Mike agreed. "I heard that name all too frequently at the reunion."

Gary's office resembled the standard banker's office with blond wood desk and credenza, a green glass shade banker's lamp on one side of the desk and trays with manila folders on the other. A computer monitor and keyboard sat on a pullout shelf on the drawer side of the desk. The wall had framed diplomas from the University of Illinois and some business school Mike had never heard of before. Interspersed were a large gold crucifix and framed picture of Jesus Christ. Arranged on the middle shelf of the credenza were gold framed photos of a pair of toddlers. A young looking woman in a winged chair, posed with the boy and girl on her lap, while Gary stood behind. The woman had rows of perfect white teeth while the kids were all gleefully flashing gap-tooth grins.

"Yeah, I can imagine," Gary said in a dismissive tone.

"I was hoping to see you at the reunion," Mike said. "They were paying tribute to our baseball team. You remember? We were the team that almost went to the state championship."

"I...I...can't go to those things," Gary said, adding flatly. "Oh, and by the way...I am sorry to hear about your wife."

"Thanks," Mike quietly replied. "How'd you know?"

"The Daily had a small story," Gary said. "How long ago was it?"

"She...died about six months ago."

"Died? I thought she was..."

"Yeah," Mike answered curtly. "She was killed."

"Man," Gary exclaimed, looking over to the pictures on the credenza. "I don't know what I would do if something happened to my Milly or the kids."

"It's rough sometimes."

"I can imagine," Gary arched forward, tapping the pen on the desk pad. "What business are you in nowadays?" He shifted topics with careless ease.

"I'm the Call Center Director for a data and research company."

Gary stared at him for a long moment, tap, tap, tapping the pen on the desk pad. Mike let out a short laugh and smiled.

"I manage the company's call centers and research locations worldwide."

Gary's eyebrows arched. "Wow. Is that a lot of travel?"

"It's not too bad," Mike said. He noticed movement on the right side of Gary's suit jacket and realized Gary's leg was twitching.

"Where do you go?" Tap, tap, tap, tap.

"Asia, England and Rockford."

"Rockford? That's exotic." Gary's voice betrayed impatience. "You must have frequent flier miles up the wazoo. Pay pretty good?" Tap, tap, tap.

"Yeah, I have tons of miles. Never get a chance to use them though," Mike said. "It does pay good, but not great."

"Is that the business you wanted to talk to me about?" Gary asked. "Want to set up an IRA?" He noticed himself tapping the pen and stopped. When he looked back and across the desk, Mike glared hard at him.

"Not really."

"Well? What then?" Gary said slowly, hesitantly, holding both hands open. His fingers were shaking.

"I was talking to Donnie at the reunion…"

"Who?" Gary interrupted. His lack of recollection didn't sound convincing.

"Inge…Donnie Inge, our right fielder…remember?" Mike pointedly said.

"I thought he was dead," Gary's voice was caustic.

"He's bruised a bit, but he's very much alive," Mike reassured him. "I thought you guys were pals from way back in Blackhawk Elementary."

"No…we were never friends." Gary snapped back.

"You hung out all the time." Mike's tone was disbelieving.

Gary said nothing, his face set.

"Yeah," Mike said. "Donnie was talking, talking a lot, and he told me an interesting story. A very interesting story," Mike said slowly.

"Donnie's a drunk," Gary interjected, picking up the pen and fidgeting again.

"He is a drunk," Mike agreed, nodding his head. "He was telling me a story about a girl I used to date...Grace House. You remember Grace?"

"I don't have time for this. I don't know who that is," Gary abruptly said, his voice quivering. Color began to rise in his neck and cheeks.

"Grace and her sister Chastity," Mike pressed on. "It was a terrible story, Gary. A really," he said slowly, "terrible story."

"I don't know what you're talking about," Gary insisted.

"No?" Mike leaned forward and stepped up his questioning. "You and Donnie were buddies, all the way up to that play-off ball game."

Gary squirmed in his chair. "Yeah, so what? We had a falling out."

"Donnie told me a lot," Mike said, adding slowly for emphasis. "A lot about what happened to Grace and Chastity, her younger sister."

"I still don't know what you're talking about," Gary protested, his voice rising. "What does this have to do with me?"

"You need to tell me what happened to Grace and her sister." Mike rose from the chair and put his hands on Gary's desk. "You need to tell me what you did."

Gary slammed the pen onto the desk. He stood, his face flushed and his eyes bulging and shifting side to side, but not looking at Mike. "If that's what you came here for, you need to leave," he said loudly.

Mike stepped back. "Easy, Gary. I was just asking you a question."

"You need to leave." Breathing heavily, beads of sweat formed on Gary's upper lip and wet lines ran down his temples.

"Relax, Gary," Mike stuck his finger out at Gary. "I want you to tell me about raping Grace...raping her and Chastity. Was it at one of Decker's parties?"

Gary's eyes flashed wide with fright, his mouth agape. "You...you have to leave...now." He stumbled, catching the corner of the desk and staggering. "I didn't have anything to do with that."

"I'm leaving, Gary," Mike relented, backing away to the door. "We'll talk again, buddy." Mike turned and briskly walked across the rotunda, through a gauntlet of questioning eyes and people with bewildered expressions. At the glass doors, Mike paused and looked back. Gary stood in the doorway to his office, his head down, rubbing his brow.

Back in his car, Mike let out a long breath and went over the exchange with Gary. Based on his reactions it was obvious Gary was involved, up to his neck. Mike opened his notebook and jotted down notes about the encounter. When done, he flipped back to the first page. Below Donnie Inge's name, Mike wrote Gary Watson. He stopped and looked out the side window. What do these two have in common, one a bank manager and the other a drunk? Growing up in Park Forest Gary and Donnie were inseparable pals from elementary though junior high and in high school at Rich High. But in senior year, with the Rich High Rockets baseball team on the day of the big game they seemed to fall out. Mike leafed to an open page and sketched a baseball diamond. He wrote Donnie in right field, himself at third base, Gary at shortstop. Who else?

Mike wrote Decker at first base. It had to be. Decker's dad and the parties, he recalled Donnie saying, it wasn't just the booze talking. Gary's reaction when he mentioned Decker's name and the parties corroborated it.

"There's too much smoke here," he muttered.

The more he thought about it the more sense it made. Donnie, Gary and Decker always hung out together. They were always arriving together, driven by Decker's dad. Mike closed the notebook. "Looks like I need to talk to Decker," he murmured to himself, turning the key in the ignition. "But first, somehow I have to talk to Grace."

As the car idled Mike pressed send on Grace's name in his phone. He let it ring and ring, fully expecting no answer. A voice came over the line.

"Grace?"

"No, this is Jeff, her husband." His tone was measured and deliberate.

"Hi Jeff, this is Mike..."

"I know who it is," Jeff interrupted. He was angry, but controlled it. "You need to stop calling Grace. You need to stop leaving messages on her phone."

"But, I need to talk to..."

"You aren't talking to her."

"But..."

"Listen, Mike. If you keep calling her and leaving messages we'll have to go to the authorities, and..."

"You don't know, do you?"

There was a pause.

"Know what?" Jeff's tone had changed.

Now Mike paused.

"Know what?" Jeff's voice sounded urgent.

"Ask...your wife," Mike said emphatically.

"Are you two...?"

Mike broke the connection. He stared at the phone for a moment. It was a shitty thing to do. "Now she'll call me," he thought, putting his phone on the passenger seat and shifting the car into drive.

As he gauged traffic on the street waiting to pull out he saw Gary hurriedly leaving the bank and going to a large tan sedan in the parking lot. He fumbled with keys, before unlocking the driver's side door and getting in. He revved the engine and backed out, anxiously looking left and right at the intersection.

Mike let a small black Fiat pull past him and eased out of the parking space, keeping his eyes on Gary's sedan ahead. "Where's he going in such a hurry?"

6

Mike hung back four car lengths. Gary turned onto Homewood Road going south. Mike accelerated through the amber light rather than lose Gary.

"C'mon, Gary, what're you up to?" Mike muttered, keeping his eye on the beige sedan.

Gary stopped at a stoplight, signaling a right turn on Flossmoor Road.

Suddenly the car between Mike and Gary turned into a parking lot. "Shit," Mike hissed, losing the cover between him and Gary. He slowed as much as he could without being conspicuous, and rolled closer and closer. Mike slunk low in the driver's seat. As he was about to brake behind Gary, the beige sedan turned right.

Too close, Mike thought. He doesn't know my car, but he might see me, he thought. Mike waited to turn even though there was a break in traffic. Once he swung into his lane, he spotted Gary ahead and kept pace.

The toney suburban neighborhoods of Homewood gave way to the even more affluent Flossmoor. It seemed as if every mile had at least one country club and expanse of golf course. Even the poorer quarters of Flossmoor had 1920s red brick homes interspersed with 1930's boxy front porch designs, or 1940s smallish and 1950s ranch styles. Here and there 1960s fake colonials interspersed with 1970s tri-levels.

Gary pulled into a parking lot in a strip mall. Mike eased into the far end of the long lot and braked in front of a package store.

Mike's phone lit up. Grace's number, but he knew it had to be Jeff. He didn't answer.

After a while a black Cadillac Seville with tinted windows and Illinois plates pulled up back to front to Gary's car. Mike could only see Gary talking, gesturing with his hands and nodding. A finger pointed out the Cadillac window, poking at Gary. Gary seemed to shrink in his seat, like a child being reprimanded. The Seville pulled away leaving Gary slumped forward with his face in his hands. Mike debated whether to pull up to Gary's car, but decided to wait, watch, and see what happened next.

Mike's phone lit up again. He glanced over. This wasn't Grace's number, nor was it work. Gary's car started moving and Mike pulled out, accelerating to catch up to Gary. The phone beeped, the call had gone to voice mail.

Staying back Mike followed Gary through Flossmoor. While driving he accessed his voice mail. He keyed in his password; there was one new message. It was a voice Mike didn't recognize.

"Mike Smith," the voice was low, deep and ominous. "You need to go back to Des Moines, cry for your dead wife and leave the past alone. Got it?"

The message shook Mike. His hands gripped the steering wheel. He grew angry and nearly lost sight of Gary's car ahead.

They passed the mock English Tudor style downtown of Flossmoor Commons and continued into the neighborhoods. The homes became larger, more and more expensive looking, some with circular drives, other homes with elaborate landscaping of hedges and trees and flower beds. Long sloping lush green lawns with large old oaks and maples rolled to street.

Gary turned into an exclusive enclave called Highland Hills alongside Coyote Run Golf Course. The wide subdivision streets wound round and round and Mike hung well back from Gary's car. From a corner Mike saw Gary pull into the driveway of a large sandy colored brick and stucco three-story house on Park Avenue. He drove to the cul-de-sac and turned around, coming back to park in front of the house. As he got out and started up the long red brick sidewalk to the front door, Mike noticed curtains in a large picture window draw back. Within seconds Gary was out the front door, down the short flight of steps and coming quickly toward Mike.

"Why are you here?" Gary almost shouted. His neck and face glowed beet red. Gary could never handle pressure. "What do you want?"

"You know what I want." Mike stopped. "I want you to tell me what you did to Grace."

"I, I don't know what you're talking about." Gary panted hard.

"I know you were part of it. Who else was involved?"

"No...I had nothing to do with it." Gary's eyes darted away, his face flushed.

Gary's young blonde wife, with a baby on her hip, opened the front door. "Gary? Are you okay?"

Mike took a side step around Gary. "Hello, Mrs. Watson." He called to her in a friendly voice, adding in a whisper to Gary, "Maybe I should ask your wife?"

Gary puts his hands out, stepping back and getting in front of Mike. "If you say a word to her I will...I will," he fumed.

Mike realized he had Gary cornered and now he would fight back. He quickly changed his tactic. "Why do you protect them?" Mike, keeping his voice in an undertone, angrily demanded. "Why should you and your family suffer for what they did to those two girls?"

Gary's hands slowly fell to his sides.

"Maybe you and your friend would like to come in for a coffee or soda?" Gary's wife asked. Her eyes darted from Gary to Mike, confused.

Mike tilted his head and caught Gary's downcast eyes. "Should we go in?" he said quietly.

"No," he replied, seeming resigned.

"We're okay, Mrs. Watson," Mike called with a wave. "That was very kind of you to offer."

Gary turned and paced, head down, pinching his upper lip.

"Gary?" Mike finally said. "You going to tell me what happened?"

"I can't. I'll lose everything, my job, my house, my wife and my family." He paused. "I owe him everything."

"And I'm supposed to pity you after what you did to Grace and her sister Chastity?"

"Why do you care? What's Grace to you?"

"It's none of your business what Grace means to me. It's a horrible thing, a crime what men do to women. I never understood that horror until they raped and killed my wife. You know what someone did to my wife is like what you did to Grace and Chastity."

Gary looked at Mike a long time. "I'm not one of them."

Staring hard at Gary and slowly, pointedly, he said "yes...you are Gary."

"You don't know how hard I have prayed..."

Mike wouldn't let him finish. "And you thought praying would cleanse you?"

"You talked to Grace?"

"Yeah," Mike replied.

Gary's face fell. "I'm so sorry about her sister."

Mike was curious. "Why? Why are you so sorry about her sister?"

"Chastity committed suicide before graduating high school."

Something like an electric shock surged through Mike. He grabbed Gary by the lapels and pushed him backward. Surprised, Gary stumbled and fell to the lawn.

"You son of a bitch," Mike yelled. "You killed her. You're responsible for that poor girl."

"Gary? Gary?" his wife leapt out the front door and down the steps with the baby crying on her hip. "What's going on? Are you okay, honey?" Then she turned on Mike. "You get out of here. Get out or I'll call the police."

Gary lay there dazed, his arm up to shield his face. "I pray," he murmured. "I pray for her every day."

"You pray for her?" Mike mocked. "You selfish son of a bitch. You only pray for yourself." Mike backed away. "Call the police," he challenged Gary's wife. "You talk to me," he said to Gary. "Or I will be back to tell her." He turned just as Gary's wife lunged and swatted at him. He went to his car, shaking with rage.

"Tell me what?" he heard Gary's wife saying to him.

Mike looked over at Gary's wife, trying to help him to his feet while holding the squalling baby. He pulled away from the curb quickly, realizing he'd let his emotions take hold and hadn't yet heard the whole story. He didn't know exactly where to go from there. As he drove out of Highland Hills he thought about what other connections there were to pursue. He had to talk to Decker. Would he get any answers? Who does Gary owe everything to? It has to be Decker, though more than likely it's Decker's dad?

The old man, Mike remembered, had small, beady blue eyes that would burn right through you when he held you in his gaze. Those soulless eyes would make Mike cringe. He recalled meeting Rod Decker's dad for the first time as he stood with a group of ball players behind the dugout.

"Just call me Sam, boys," he said in a reedy voice, pulling tight his thin white lips.

The forced familiarity always made Mike uneasy around the old man.

Short, with a wiry frame, he stood only a head above the chain link fence surrounding the ball field as he watched the games. He always wore a grey or dark blue suit; and on hot days he would loosen his tie, roll up the sleeves of his white shirt and expose freckled pasty white arms. Sam Decker showed for every practice and every game. Years before Sam Decker had been the principal of Rich High, but then he had moved up to the vice superintendent of Park Forest schools.

Sam wasn't one of the loud fathers, bellowing from the stands at their son to 'get your back elbow up' when batting, or 'make the play' when out in the field. Nor did he live vicariously his own failed sports career through his son like other dads. He almost ignored his own son Rod. Sam Decker only wanted to be one of the guys. He would buy favor with hot dogs, candy and sodas and swear using the latest slang. But he especially liked to talk to the guys about the girls in the stands. He would point out girls and say "she's a cutie. You want me to go and tell her you want to take her out?"

Mike's dad and mom had little interest in sports and would only occasionally attend a game. They didn't discourage him; they just weren't interested. Sam Decker noticed this and went out of his way to befriend Mike. Mike would be joking with the guys after a game and suddenly Sam Decker would be next to him, laughing at a joke he hadn't heard. Though polite, it was awkward and Mike avoided Sam Decker as much as possible.

Now that he recalled, Sam Decker had asked him about Grace, staring at her in the stands and asking "is that your girlfriend, Mike?" Chastity went to some of the games with Grace. "Is that her little sister?" the old man asked.

Connected politically and financially, Sam Decker easily climbed the ladder to state office. There were always photos in the Park Forest Daily of Sam Decker posing a 'grab and grin' with some high-ranking downstate politician. The people Sam Decker didn't agree with often were never heard from again. From Park Forest he went to superintendent of Cook County schools and then to the capitol in Springfield.

He's got to be in his eighties now, Mike thought. That is if he is still alive.

And now he knew why Grace wouldn't talk about her sister Chastity.

Spring break and Mike relished the lull between the exhausting winter term and upcoming hectic spring term. His first year at Southern Illinois had been scramble and confusion at the outset. From finding himself in the wrong building in the wrong classroom for the wrong course and trying to sneak out without being seen; to the loud and nonstop chaos of dorm life, he had grown. Back at home on Blackhawk Drive, Park Forest, his room with the sports trophies, old toys, comic books and faded pictures seemed small. His mother, happy to see him and glad to be useful when he dumped double bags of laundry by the washing machine, became distressed when she caught him doing laundry and cooking his own dinner. His father just smiled from his overstuffed chair, watching Mike over the top of his evening newspaper, keeping his distance.

Mike no longer fit.

He walked at night revisiting boyhood haunts. Sitting on a bench in the shadows to the left of the bright entrance to Rudy's Market, Mike sipped a warm café au lait watching the rush of traffic at the intersection of Sauk Trail and Blackhawk Drive. His green Rich High letterman's jacket kept the late March chill away. Remembering riding his bicycle to the large blue Quonset hut-styled market for candy, baseball cards or the latest comic books with his weekly paper route pay in his pocket gave Mike peace. At this moment heavy textbooks, early morning lectures, late night study and next term's full class schedule was somewhere south, in Carbondale.

A Pontiac Trans-Am's dual exhaust growled and snarled like a prowling beast, swerving into Rudy's parking lot. Grey primer splotched the faded black paint of the two-door muscle car. Chrome mag wheels gleamed in the light. The windows were down and AC/DC's *Highway to Hell* blasted from the stereo.

I'm on the Highway to Hell...
Highway to Hell...

Revving up the V-8, the driver shut down the engine and headlights. A smallish girl rode shotgun. As she opened the door the backseat passenger pushed the seat back forward and climbed out. Squashed to the dashboard, the girl loudly protested. "Damn it, Willy."

Willy laughed. He was tall with shoulder length greasy black hair and dressed in black from his engineer's boots, jeans and t-shirt to his silver studded motorcycle jacket. Mike figured he was in his mid to late twenties. The driver got out the other side. He also seemed in his late twenties and dressed entirely in black, but for his long scraggly blonde hair. He bent forward, then quickly straightened up flipping his long hair back.

"I need smokes, Bobby," the girl in the front seat called out.

"We're getting beer. You want smokes come get'em yourself."

"What kind we getting, Shits, I mean Schlitz?"

The thin girl stepped out the passenger side. She had a floppy mop of teased ginger hair and stood half the height of Willy and easily ten years younger than both men. Her face had been heavily made up and that must've been a while ago. Her black panda eyes had streaked down to her cheeks and red lipstick smeared across one cheek.

Mike recognized her right off.

Willy saw Mike sitting on the bench. "What're you looking at, fruit?"

Bobby and the girl turned.

"I'm not a fruit." Mike got up.

The girl smiled a tough girl grin. "Hey, Mike."

"Hi Chastity," he said.

"You know this guy?"

"Wait," Bobby said. "I know you. You're that ball player. He's no fruit, Willy."

Chastity wore skin tight black hip-hugger jeans with a chain belt and a Motorhead War Pig t-shirt with cut-off sleeves, cut-off collar and high at the midriff showing her belly. She had on spike heels, black patent leather shining in the light. Standing with her hands on her hips and hips cocked to one side she looked Mike up and down. Her mouth was parted, her pink tongue slowly wetting her upper lip from corner to corner.

"Chastity? I thought your name was C'mere." Willy walked around the front of the Trans-Am, chuckling. He and Bobby started for the entrance.

"What kind of smokes you want, babe?"

"You know I smoke Marlboros. Hard pack," she added.

Mike walked up to her. He fought a quiver in his belly.

"Thought you were in college."

"I am. Southern Illinois. It's Spring Break."

"What're you wearing that letterman's jacket for?" Chastity took a half step forward and reaching out with black painted nails, lightly traced the large embroidered letter R on the breast of his jacket.

"I was cold."

"I know better ways to stay warm." She tilted her head and smirked, slowly rocking her hips side to side.

Mike realized she was toying with him. In a crude way she exercised the power women possess over men, the catnip few cats can resist. "Aren't you still in school?"

She turned away exhaling loudly. "Yes. I'll be a junior next year. So?"

"So? What're you...16? How old are those guys?"

"None of your business." she pulled a crushed red and white pack of Marlboros from her back pocket and pinched out the last bent cigarette. She held it up between two fingers. "You got a light?"

"I don't smoke. Those gearheads have to be ten or fifteen years older than you."

"I told you, it's none of your business. Bobby's fun and he can buy beer and...."

"Maybe it isn't my business but what happened to the kid sister always tagging along with me and Grace to bowling and ball games? Remember the time we took you to the Holiday Theatre to see *Alien*. Your mom wouldn't let you go. We told her it was a Disney movie. You were so scared—but you loved it."

Chastity took a lighter from her jeans pocket and lit her cigarette. She blew the smoke into Mike's face. He backed away. She laughed. "That chick's gone. She doesn't live here anymore."

"That girl was going to marry Donny Osmond. She had posters of Michael Jackson on her bedroom wall. She was an A student in school and going to college."

Her mouth twisted into a teasing smile, with veiled eyes Chastity regarded Mike. She had her left arm across her waist and right elbow resting on it. The cigarette in her right hand curled smoke up into the overhead lights of the parking lot.

"What happened to you, Sweet Pea?"

"Don't call me that," she snapped, taking a drag. "I got religion."

"Religion, huh?" Mike sighed. "How's Grace?"

"I was wondering when you were going to ask me about Grace."

"What's she doing?"

"At home...washing her hair."

"She okay?"

The pneumatic doors opened and Bobby and Willy came out of Rudy's with the store manager on their heels. Bobby had a six pack of Schlitz in one hand, a paper bag in the other.

"Hey, man," Willy said loudly, with his arms outstretched. "I didn't steal nothing. You want to search me? Try. You lay a finger on me and I'll kick your ass from the produce aisle to the meat department. You'll look like a heap of hamburger when I'm done with you."

"Clean up on aisle four." Bobby ducked his head and spun around on his heels, unable to stop from laughing.

The manager said something in a low squeaky voice, poking his finger at Willy, then at Bobby.

"Fuck you," Willy shot back. "We'll come here anytime we want. We'll see ya tomorrow."

They sauntered back to the Trans-Am, chuckling.

"You got my smokes?"

"Hell yeah," Bobby said, reaching down into the front of his black jeans. He pulled out a couple red and white packs and showed them to Chastity. She smiled.

"See, I didn't steal nothing," Willy said.

"Want a beer, ball player?"

Mike held up his white Styrofoam cup. "I'm good."

"That ain't beer."

"Don't stand...don't stand...don't stand so close to him," Bobby half-sang.

"Yeah, baby, you stand there any longer he'll be turning Japanese," Willy opened the door of the Trans-Am.

"You really think so?" Bobby chimed in.

"Tell your sister I said hello," Mike said as Chastity skipped back to the car.

"Tell her yourself."

"I can't do that," Mike said.

"Call me," Chastity said as she stepped into the Trans-Am.

Mike shook his head.

"Hey? Chastity?" He went up to the car as Bobby turned over the ignition and the Trans-Am roared to life. *Highway to Hell* blasted. At the window Mike leaned in. Chastity popped the top of a can of Schlitz. "Why did Grace break up with me?"

"Hands off the car ball player."

"Yeah, go play with your balls," Willy said.

Chastity slurped white beer foam off the top of the can. She gazed at Mike with a serious expression on her face. "It's a secret." For an instant, Mike glimpsed lil Sweet Pea in Chastity's sad eyes.

Just then Bobby burned rubber backing out. He wheeled the powerful Pontiac around. The tires threw smoke from the wheel wells as he accelerated onto Sauk Trail.

What secret?

This was the last time he saw Chastity. And until today he hadn't known she killed herself.

There were missed calls on his phone, all Grace's number. The threatening voice mail still bothered Mike. That voice on his phone gave him pause. He'd heard the voice before. A lot of things had been set in motion and Mike thought maybe he should get out of the area for now.

Mike headed south, to pick up I-80 and then I-355 north into the west suburbs. There was a lot of time to think and a lot of things to think about. He didn't want to think about it right then, so he turned on sports talk radio and let the voices bickering back and forth over the terrible Cubs, frustrating White Sox, triumphant Bulls or bewildering Bears distract him. Suburbs gave way to long stretches of farm lands, with corn, soy or wheat crops, in mid-summer growth. After Aurora he exited onto I-39 north toward Rockford. He would reach the call center just after lunch. They might be surprised at his visit, but he would take a temporary office and fill in more in the notebook.

Mike spent the night in Rockford, deciding to swing back to Flossmoor the next day and pay a visit to Gary Watson's young wife. He could time it so Gary would be at work. That might put pressure on Gary if he learned Mike was talking to his wife. Schaumburg was on the way and Mike had an opportunity to stop at St. Peter's.

Every chance he got, he went to see Becky. Professionals said he wasn't adjusting like he should. The counselor advised him to allow the process to work, let it unfold naturally. It was all Mike could do to keep his mouth shut and tell the counselor there was nothing natural about any of this and he had all he could handle to stay sane and not drown in the sadness his life had become. "Leave me alone," he mumbled to himself. "I will work through it in my own time and in my own way."

He left Rockford early, reaching Schaumburg at around 8:30 in the morning. He exited I-90 and picked up East Schaumburg road. Late commute traffic scattered the roadway, but no delays. He approached the mock colonial sandy stone of St. Peter's Lutheran church with its three red doors, three stained glass windows, towering New England style steeple, and adjacent cemetery. The tall, arched black wrought iron gates were drawn back, opening to the rolling green hills and tree lined shady lanes of the cemetery. Mike slowly pulled into the gravel parking lot.

St. Peter's Lutheran was the oldest cemetery in Schaumburg, dating back to 1847. It held the gravesites of many of the founding families of Schaumburg. There were large ornate granite markers for the Nerge and Lengl families, and a stone mausoleum for the Winkelhake clan.

Mike stepped out of his car and took a deep breath. Cars clustered in one corner of the parking lot. The sun lay low, but burned warm and bright, with a few puffy white clouds lazing across the pale blue horizon. Mike's shoes loudly crunched on the gravel as he crossed the parking lot and entered the cemetery grounds.

People act differently in a cemetery. They move with wary lethargy, with bowed head and speak in muted tones. A mother and her two children walked by, flowers in hand. They were dressed well, the boy in a navy blue suit, the girl in a grey dress with white collar and gloves, the mother in black dress, black hat and veil. Mike looked past them and saw a burial party gathering on a far hilltop.

Passing large monuments and family plots, in and out of the shade of a large canopy of trees, Mike trudged up a paved walkway and turned left at a well rutted pathway to the Devereux' family plot. He paused at the grouping of stones. There were rows of faded and weatherworn headstones. These slabs honored the 19th century

Devereux', those who settled in the Schaumburg area. Becky's memorial rested one plot beyond her father, who had a fatal heart attack when she was in her teens. The newest stone, still shiny dark marble bore the engraving Rebecca Devereux Smith: beloved daughter, wife and mother, with the brief epitaph *Taken Too Soon*. Three fresh white roses in a vase were set to the side of the headstone. Mike knew his mother-in-law had visited, as she did each week.

He went down to a knee, reached out and placed his hand softly on the cool dew wet grass where he imagined Becky's heart lay. "I'm here, Becks," he whispered.

It had been such a battle with Becky's mother to have her buried in the family plot at St. Peter's. A stubborn woman, she was used to getting her way. She barely disguised her contempt for Mike. She argued that with his traveling, like a common brush salesman, and his call centers in dirty little countries around the world, his prospects for the Board Room were limited. "The telephone operator," she sniffed, intimating he was beneath her daughter. Mike's career certainly didn't compare well with Becky's father and the Devereux', who for generations rode the big shoulders of the Chicago Mercantile Exchange.

Mike couldn't summon the strength to battle with Madame Devereux. He called her Madame despite Becky's objections. The events of Becky's death had shattered Mike. And so, she was laid to rest for all eternity in the Devereux' family plot. Mike looked to the open space to Becky's left. There was room for one more plot. Madame Devereux had already made it quite clear the plot was reserved for her favorite grandson Spencer, a Devereux through and through. As Becky's brother had daughters, Spencer was the eldest and only male among the grandkids and received more attention and monetary blessings from the grand dame.

Becky's mother was, of course, a Devereux by marriage. She claimed lineage from the Spencer and Kent families, original settlers of Northern Illinois and the area when it was known as Sarah's Cove. Though, her claim couldn't be confirmed. Mike's parents were middleclass, not unusual and turned from the common cloth. They loved Becky as much as they loved Mike. His mom was in complete awe and fear of the elder Mrs. Devereux. She would alternately praise the woman and turn white with fright in her presence. Mike's dad, the quiet man he was, lived by the adage if you haven't anything nice to say about someone, say nothing. Consequently, he rarely spoke about Mrs. Devereux.

"It doesn't matter, darling," he could hear Becky saying. "I love you."

"I know," Mike murmured. "I miss you so much."

She knew that.

"Becks," he started. "I've got myself messed up in something awful and I'm not sure why I'm compelled to get involved."

A short, white-haired man with a stooped walk, hands clasped behind his back, shambled past. He wore a long charcoal grey drape coat with black velvet collar. Atop his round head he wore a high crown, stiff brim Boss of the Plains hat made of black beaver felt. His head hung down and he seemed deep in thought, as if wrestling with the worries of the world. Self-conscious, Mike waited for him to pass.

"I don't know what the outcome will be," he continued in a low voice. "I can't help you, but maybe I can help someone else." Mike took a deep breath. "I love you, Becks. I miss you so much."

He struggled up, wiping his eyes and gazing down at her. Even now, six months later, he couldn't believe she lay there, forever gone. "I've got to go," he said, bending and kissing the cold and roughhewn top of Becky's headstone. "I'll be back next week. I love you."

Mike walked slowly back down the pathway. He had the sensation he forgot something. Reaching the parking lot he turned and looked to Becky's resting place. The old man in the Boss of the Plains hat stood at her headstone, the sun shining at his shoulder.

7

Morning shone bright as Mike drove out of Schaumburg southeast to Flossmoor. Recalling from yesterday, Mike located Coyote Run Golf Course and Highland Hills' upscale enclave. He drove up Park Avenue and slowed by the house and turned around at the cul-de-sac. Mike parked out front. Pausing a moment he surveyed the three-story sandy colored brick and stucco house and grounds. Well-kept and professionally landscaped, Mike doubted Gary sweat Saturday mornings pushing the mower up and back, up and back.

Gary's beige sedan wasn't parked in the drive and the curtains were open. Mike went up the walk to the front door, took off his sunglasses and rang the bell. He heard a commotion inside, a child shouting and a female voice telling the kid not to answer the door. After a short while, the lock clattered and the door partially opened.

"Hello?" Guarded in tone, Mike realized she recognized him from yesterday. A small blonde girl ran up behind her and peeked around her legs. "You were here yesterday...with Gary."

"Yes," Mike said, flashing a smile. "It's Milly, isn't it? Is Gary here?"

"No. I'm sorry, Gary's not here."

"Not here? I'm confused," Mike responded, touching his head. "Gary told me last night to meet him here...this morning."

"You talked to Gary last night?"

"Yeah," Mike said. "We had that unfortunate misunderstanding yesterday and were going to sort it out this morning. He said to meet him here at..." Mike glanced at his watch. "At 10:30 this morning."

Milly's apprehension vanished as Mike's explanation of yesterday's confrontation sufficed. She smiled, relieved. "Well, maybe Gary's on his way home from work." She shuffled back, scooting the little girl to the side, opening the door wide. "Honey, back up. Would you like to come in and wait for Gary?"

"That's very kind of you." He stepped up and over the threshold. "I sure would."

"We could wait out on the patio," Milly said, closing the door after Mike. "Would you like some tea, coffee, maybe lemonade?"

"Lemonade would great. Thank you."

"Just go through the living room," she pointed. "And then the dining room to the patio. I'll be out in a jiffy with some lemonade."

"Sure." Mike walked through the living room. Sunlight filled the room, decorated with a beige and white brocade couch and matching chairs. In a corner playpen the youngest Watson, a blond boy still in diapers, sat gnawing on a wet rubber toy. An inordinately large framed portrait of Jesus in varying soft shades of brown and gold hung over the white fireplace mantle. Jesus' blue eyes followed Mike across the room. Ornate brass crucifixes flanked the portrait, family photos and Gary and his wife's wedding picture, lined the mantle. The photos looked familiar. Mike realized he had seen the same framed collection in Gary's office at the bank yesterday. Open on a lectern stood an bible next to a white bookcase with few books and an array of religious paraphernalia. Mike could hear Gary's wife in the kitchen and the little girl constantly asking questions about the visitor. Gary's wife shushed her and reminded her it was not polite to ask so many questions.

Mike slid the patio door aside and stepped outside onto the patio. The sun was bright and Mike took out his sunglasses and put them on. He pulled a chair from under a wire mesh patio table shaded by a tilted tan umbrella. The small, but nicely manicured backyard with red, yellow and white rose bushes along a white picket fence and bushes in the corners was flooded by sunlight. A single tree maybe about 12 feet tall, neatly rounded, stood off to the side in the center of a rock lined mound of new mulch. A child's plastic swimming pool with about three or four inches of water, was in the sunny corner of the patio. Children's toys floated in the water.

Milly, holding a tray of glasses and a pitcher of pink lemonade with ice, struggled to open the patio door. She waited for the little girl to follow her out. "C'mon, sweetie," she urged the small child.

Mike went saying "let me take that," took the tray and placed it in the center of the wire mesh table.

"Thank you," Gary's wife said, breathlessly collapsing into a chair. She patted either cheek with the back of her hand and let out a sigh. "You will have to forgive me but I don't recall your name and how you know Gary." She poured pink lemonade and clattering ice cubes into a glass.

Mike chuckled. "You're forgiven. I'm not sure we were formally introduced. I'm Mike, Mike Smith. I know Gary from Rich High, the baseball team."

"Oh yes," Milly said, remembering. "That ol' baseball team." The little girl running over to the play pool distracted her. "Donna...Donna, come back over here by mommy. I have some lemonade for you." The little girl reluctantly came back and stood half hidden at her mother's hip. Donna stared at Mike with big curious eyes and a finger in her mouth.

Mike took the glass of cool lemonade Gary's wife offered. He drank and studied her a moment over the top of the glass. She had short blonde hair flipped below the ears with a white band holding most of the hair back except for bangs. She wore a orange and white flower print shift showing her pasty white arms. To say she was plain looking would be unfair. Milly had nice skin and common blonde Nordic looks. Mike knew she was young, but with her round cheeks she looked extremely young, twenties for sure, perhaps barely in her mid-twenties.

"Do you know my daddy?" the little girl asked.

"Sure do, sweetie," Mike said. "We played baseball together."

"Baseball?" the girl said, laughing. "My daddy doesn't play baseball."

"Maybe not now, but he used to play. And he was pretty good too."

Milly giggled. "Oh, he's always going on about that team almost going to the state championship."

"It was a good team," Mike said, taking a drink. "Just fell a couple runs shy to get to the state championship."

"Gary still goes to see Mr. Decker, twice a month. They play cards at Mr. Decker's house."

Mike swallowed quickly. "Really? They play poker?"

"Oh no, not gambling—that would be a sin," Milly said, her hand on her chest. "They play hearts. Sometimes they get to playing hearts that Gary just forgets the time. He comes in very early and is very tired the next morning." She laughed, drinking. "He thinks I'll be mad that he's coming in so late, but they're just boys being boys."

"You got that right, boys being boys," Mike said under his breath.

Gary's wife face scrounged up. "If you're old friends, why were you two fighting yesterday?"

"Fighting? No, it was nothing like that," Mike assured her. "We just had a misunderstanding about a business matter. I think I accidentally bumped him."

"And you boys did makeup?"

"Yes, we did," Mike assured her with a grin. "Why else would he ask me to meet him here today?"

The baby inside the house started crying and Gary's wife jumped to her feet and darted into the house. Mike looked at little Donna. She was as blonde as her mother but a bit disheveled. She now had two fingers in her mouth, staring at him from behind the chair.

"Is your daddy nice to you?" Mike asked her.

She nodded.

"Don't let daddy be too nice," he added. The little girl looked at him not understanding.

Milly was back with the baby on her hip. "I'm so sorry. Orel is just a little fussy today."

"That's alright," Mike said, as she sat down. "I don't think Gary has ever told me, but where did you two meet?"

Gary's wife wiped drool off the boy's chin and t-shirt with a pleased smile at Mike's question. "It was in church, which is not surprising." She looked down demurely. "Gary is such a strong man of God. That's what attracted me to him. Other than Jesus he is my rock."

Mike listened, sipping lemonade. "He taught Sunday School, didn't he?" he asked.

"Oh my yes," Milly seemed surprised. "How ever did you know that?"

"I think I know Gary," Mike replied. "He always liked the young ones."

"Yes," she enthused. "He really connected with our tiny disciples."

"Especially the little girls, I bet."

"You do know our Gary," she beamed with pride. "The young ladies loved Gary like a big brother. He would try to be fair but always had his favorite girls. He said he loved to see them bloom and blossom."

"Oh yeah," Mike agreed. "We know our Gary."

"And I don't for the life of me understand why some of the girls would turn their back on Gary and seem afraid of him when they got a little older. After all he did for those girls. It's very sad."

Mike had heard enough. He pulled out his phone. "I wonder if Gary forgot our meeting," he said to Milly. "I'll give him a call." He pretended to scroll down the screen and feigned pressing SEND, putting the phone to his ear. "Gary Watson, please," he said into the phone. "He may be on his way right now," Mike said as an aside to Gary's wife. "Hey Gary, it's Mike," he said as if talking to Gary on the phone. "I thought we were meeting at your house this morning." He paused, letting it seem Gary was replying. "So..." He waited. "So...we can meet next week then?" Mike was quiet. "Okay...you betcha, I'll tell her. See ya, buddy." Mike squinted at the phone.

"Is everything alright?" Milly asked.

"Yeah," Mike said, sighing, taking a drink. "He got hung up with something at the bank and won't be able to get back."

"That happens all the time," Gary's wife laughed.

"We'll meet next week at the bank," Mike drained his glass of lemonade. "He wanted me to tell you he was sorry he didn't tell you about our meeting." Mike stood up. "I think I should get going. Thank you Mrs. Watson for the lemonade and wonderful company."

"Please, Mike, it's Milly. And you are so welcome," she replied, gently bouncing baby Orel on her lap.

"I enjoyed our talk," Mike said, moving to the patio door.

"I did as well," Milly got up, tucking the baby on her hip. She and little Donna followed Mike through the living room. Jesus watched. "Gary will pester me until I tell him what we talked about."

Mike paused at the door. "Let him know we had a nice afternoon." He stepped down to the walk. "Bye now," he said, as he walked to his car.

"God bless you. Bye," Milly said.

"Bye Bye," little Donna added, waving a wet hand.

Circling around to the driver's side of his car Mike had to let loose a chuckle. "Hearts," he muttered. Levity left his voice as he jerked open the car door and growled "and Sunday School girls. You bastard."

8

The four hour drive back to West Des Moines wearied Mike. He pulled into town and onto his tree-lined street. As he approached his small ranch house, he noticed a car with Illinois plates parked in front. It was a blue Japanese model coupe, riding low and tricked out with detailing and flashy chrome wheel rims. Mike turned into his driveway and saw the silhouettes of two men sitting in the car. The doors of the blue car opened as Mike turned off his engine. The men got out. The driver had a brown complexion and was short, thin, with a shaved head, black goatee and Fu Manchu mustache. He wore a wife beater t-shirt and oversized black jeans. Tattoos went up his arms to his neck. He looked Hispanic. The other, a black man well over six feet tall, appeared wide and heavyset even though he wore a baggy white striped black track pants, a red Chicago Bulls t-shirt and White Sox cap worn askew. The large black man shuffled behind the small Hispanic as they crossed the long grass of the lawn toward Mike.

Mike picked up his notebook and overnight bag.

"H-h-hey, *cabron*," the Hispanic said, getting close.

"Yeah?" Mike tried to play nonchalant. "What do you want?"

The Hispanic stopped, spat through his front teeth, spread his feet and put his hands on his hips. He was about a half a foot shorter than Mike. The black man came up behind keeping his eye on Mike. Overweight, so overweight his face seemed all fat round cheeks and double chins, with tiny eye holes and a slit for a mouth.

"We haf a message fer jew," the Hispanic said, pointing up at Mike's face.

"Me? Why me?"

"Jew shud stop asking questions or jew and jer wife will be bach togeder." A twisted smile crossed his face, he thought himself clever for saying that.

"What's that supposed to mean?" Mike shot back, shifting the overnight bag to the front, just in case.

"Um jes de messenger, man. Jew nee to tink about it," he emphasized, prodding his finger into Mike's overnight bag.

"Who sent you?" Mike asked.

"Ah liddle birdy," the Hispanic said. The black man giggled.

"Get the fuck off my property."

"Wooooooooo. I'm chakin' *cabron*."

Both turned and ambled back to the car.

"*Chinga tu madre*...Who sent you?"

"Jew jes tink, *cabron*," the little man shouted standing at the blue car, tapping his finger on the side of his head. They got in and drove off.

Mike's hand shook as he slid the key into the front door lock. He closed the heavy oak door and fell back against it, letting out a shuttering breath. The living room was dark and quiet, except for the loud tick of the mantle clock. The voice mail, these two men; there was no doubt it was because of the questions he was asking about the Grace and Chastity's rape. He had hit a nerve and that nerve twitched.

His composure regained, Mike snapped on the living room lights. Two lamps on end tables on either side of the couch cast a soft yellow light across the room. Mike dropped his bag and notebook on the couch and went into the kitchen. He flipped on the overhead light. On the counter was a pile of junk mail, circulars and unopened letters addressed to Becky Smith, Rebecca Smith and Mrs. Mike Smith. He just couldn't bring himself to open the letters. The refrigerator was covered with pictures of Becky, smiling, younger, vital, laughing and alive. A picture of her with a much taller Spencer wishing him Happy Birthday next to an older picture of Mike and Spencer, arm and arm in better times. On a dry mark calendar from last month were the days marked for his travel schedule: Manchester, Gurgaon and Rockford—then the 15th, marked '6 months'. He hadn't erased it.

He plucked a bottle of Sierra Nevada pale ale from a six-pack in the refrigerator and went to a drawer for an opener. A long pull on the cold beer helped settle his nerves after the confrontation out front.

Echoes of Becky were everywhere, not just the pictures on the refrigerator. There were pictures of her on the fireplace mantle, family pictures, a picture of Becky making a funny face standing under the Eiffel Tower and another on the beach in California. Limantour Beach, Mike remembered, Sonoma County on a drive up Highway 1 to Mendocino. He could never take those pictures down. Every time he came home he went back to a time lost. Friends, counselors, suggested he sell the house. But no, he could never. By the bay window and breakfast nook, Mike clicked on messages on the answer machine. Grace's voice surprised him.

"Michael," she started slowly. She didn't sound angry. "I know you think you are doing me a favor—righting a wrong. But you've really upset Jeff. He doesn't understand and is very insecure. He thinks we're having an affair." Silent, a long time, she continued. "I'm Mrs. Jeff Jordan now, and have been for nearly 25 years. We have a family. We're happy. I'm happy. They don't know what happened to Grace House. They don't know why Chastity died. Sometimes...things that are wrong can never be made right no matter what you do. Once it is past, life goes on. It should stay in the past and never be spoken of again. That's what I wanted. That's what Chastity wanted. We promised to never talk about it. I don't know why you are asking questions. I think it's because of what happened to your wife." Suddenly her voice sped up, as if startled. "You have forced me and we will have to meet and..." The machine beeped. The message ended.

Mike went to the next message. It was work and then no more.

He drank again and looked out the window at the backyard. Like the front lawn, the grass needed cutting. He had been neglecting his life. What had he started? How would it play out? There was no way he could let it go now. The threats didn't matter. Nor did it matter he had upset Grace and Jeff. He was determined to follow this to its resolution.

Mike called Grace, but again got voice mail. "Grace," he said. "I got your message and will meet you...and Jeff, if you like, any time. Call me back and let me know when and where we can get together."

Mike held his phone in his hand for a long time. He debated if he should call Spencer. With the two hour time difference he would be just home from work. The last time they talked, two months ago, it had been difficult. He scrolled down his contacts and pressed SEND on the Washington state phone number.

The line rang once, twice, thrice and then Spencer answered. "Hi dad," he said in a slow and unenthused voice.

"Hey, Spencer," Mike replied, summoning up some excitement in his tone. "How have you been?"

"Fine. Fine. Why are you calling, Dad?"

"Well, ah, it's been a couple of months since we last talked," Mike said in a rush. "I was just wondered how you've been doing."

A pause.

"Like I said, fine." Spencer audibly sighed.

"Work okay?"

"Work's okay.'

"Still dating that gal from Vancouver?"

"I don't want to talk about my dates," he said peevishly.

They were quiet.

"Oh, ah okay."

"Why are you calling, Dad?"

"I...just wanted to see how you were doing?"

"Hello then," Spencer said with just a hint of sarcasm, adding, "and how's your work going?"

"Good. It's real good." Like a starving man finding food, Mike grabbed for the opportunity to talk. "I just got back from India." He warmed to the change of subject. "Hey, I got a funny story."

"I don't have time for a funny story, Dad."

"No, no, you'll like this story," Mike said, enthused. "I'm flying out of India on Air India and first, we're sitting for two hours on the tarmac at IGI. It's 120 degrees outside and we're sitting there with no A/C, perspiring. Even the A/C units were dripping. So we..."

"I don't have...."

"We finally get into the air." Mike ignored Spencer's objections. "I have to make a connection in Frankfurt and with the two hour delay I'll be cutting it close."

"Dad?"

"About mid-flight I see the cabin crew coming down the aisle carrying what I thought was a sack of potatoes. But I see a blue turban unraveling and realize it's some Sikh guy that's sick or passed out or something. They pass by me and I see the guy's blank stare. His face is blue and he's barefoot. I realize he's deader than a doornail." Mike laughed. "I'm thinking two hours on the tarmac and they're dying in first class."

"Dad...I don't have..." Spencer tried again.

"They clear the middle seats of the last row and lay the guy out. They cross his arms on his chest, but don't cover his face with a sheet or anything." Again, Mike chuckles at his own story. "So every time I go to the lavatory in the back of the plane I see this guy laying there, arms crossed, and dead eyes. I start a conversation with him. Hey, terrible flight, innit?" Mike laughs out loud.

"Dad!" Spencer shouted.

"What?" Mike was startled. "What's the matter? Didn't you think that was a funny story?"

"No, not really, dad," Spencer quieted down. "Why did you call?"

"Well, I, ah," Mike stammered. He couldn't say he was lonely. "I wanted to talk to you. I, ah, wanted to know if you were coming home for Thanksgiving or Christmas."

Silence again.

"We talked about this before," Spencer picked up the conversation. "It's still too soon for me. It would be hard for me to be back in the house."

"Yeah," Mike quietly agreed. "How do you think it is for me?"

"I know how difficult it is for you. Besides," Spencer said, "Grandmother Devereux asked me to come to Schaumburg for Christmas. I can't take the time off work for more than one trip this year."

Mike said nothing.

"Have the cops caught the guys that killed mom yet?" Spencer asked.

"No, not yet. I got a call from some detective a couple of weeks ago. They are following up on leads. But they don't have any suspects yet."

"And dad," Spencer said. "You and I still have an issue between us."

"Spencer," Mike started to explain. "I just couldn't let them open the casket."

"That was my mother," Spencer's voice rose.

"You don't know what they did to her," Mike quickly said.

"I wanted to say good-bye." Spencer was angry.

"You didn't see her," Mike choked up. "I saw her in the morgue. You, you have no idea what they did to her." His hand went to his face. He couldn't stop a sudden sob.

"That...was...my...mother."

"Yes," Mike said trying to disguise his crying jags. "I didn't want that to be the last image you have of her. You don't understand..."

"No, dad," Spencer said calming down, taking a deep breath. "You don't understand," he was calmer. "But it's just going to take me a long time to accept that. Okay?"

"Yeah, I guess. Even your grandmother agreed to keep the casket closed."

"Well that's a first," Spencer said.

Mike snorted a short laugh. "Isn't that the truth."

"I know it's months away, Dad, but come out to Schaumburg at Christmas. We can get together then."

"Your grandmother didn't invite me."

"Well, I did. We have to deal with this in our separate ways, Dad. We're going to be okay, given time."

"I know that, son. And you know that I love you."

"I really do have to wrap this up, Dad."

"The gal from Vancouver?"

"Not funny, Dad."

"I know, I know." Mike paused. "One last thing, Spencer...I have some stuff going on and I'm not sure how it will turn out. Things may end..."

"What's going on, Dad?" Spencer sounded concerned.

"Nothing really. I'm fine." Mike spoke quickly. "I just wanted to call to see how you were doing. Listen, you gotta go. We, ah, we're okay, right?" Mike's upbeat tone rang false.

"Are you sure, you're okay?"

"Yeah, yeah, I'm okay. Don't worry about me. I'll talk to you later. Love ya, son."

"Love you too, Dad. Circle Christmas. We're getting together. It'll be easier for us to talk."

"Yes. Bye, Spencer." Mike clicked off the call. He laid the phone on the table, sometimes sniffing and wiping his eyes with his shirtsleeve.

A week went by and Mike didn't hear back from Grace. He didn't want to push it for fear of her changing her mind.

He went to work and tried to put the events and investigation of the past weeks out of his mind. He looked at pictures of Becky in his small office and lost himself to memories and waves of sadness. With great effort that he would pull himself out of bed in the morning. An unshakeable depression weighed on him. Diving back into hiring issues at the Delhi call center and allocating new projects for Rockford and sending ftp files to Manchester distracted him. And for moments he almost forgot Becky as he pondered who had abducted and raped Grace and her sister. By late in the day, downtime when the office went quiet and most people were home with their family, Mike would sit with a cup of coffee dwelling on what he had found out.

Over and over he would play it out in his mind. Two young girls, coming from the Aqua Center, were taken from the Park Forest Plaza. A group of youths and possibly an older man snatched the two, then went somewhere and gang raped them. The rape had never been reported. Were Grace and her sister threatened if they did report it? Donnie said some at school knew about it. Grace and Chastity were social outcasts. They still snub Grace, like that woman at the reunion. Who knew? Talk can go up and down a high school hallway quicker than a fire drill. Why was it he never heard? Only a drunk like Donnie would be so tactless to take pleasure in telling him. Chastity committed suicide. The trauma of the rape, did that drive her to it? Mike recalled seeing her in Park Forest with the two older guys. She had changed dramatically. Perhaps the fear of getting up in front of all those people for her diploma pushed her over the edge. Donnie and Gary were part of it. Gary acted scared. Rod Decker, and likely his dad, old Sam Decker, were also involved. The thought disgusted Mike. The rapes happened sometime before his Rich High baseball team played in the regional game, on the verge of going to the state championships. Mike remembered Donnie, Gary and Rod drunk, hung over or on something, playing piss-poor and costing Rich High the game.

The threats? Donnie or Gary lacked the balls make a threat, let alone back it up. The black Cadillac that met Gary in the strip mall parking lot, who was that?

Mike had to find out more and Gary could be coerced into talking. He knew Gary's wife would tell him Mike dropped by. Gary'd go crazy.

Ceiling lights in the office had been partially turned off. Cold and stale now, Mike threw his coffee cup into the garbage. Cleaners emptied trashcans and vacuumed around cubicles. An email popped up on Mike's computer screen. The Rockford Call Center was having more issues with its VoIP and need supervision. Mike sighed and replied, asking about the issues--connectivity. Mike wrote back asking if the center had contacted IT. They had not. It was late Friday and they didn't expect a response from IT. Mike thought a moment; then wrote back to send the associates home early and shut down the center for tonight. "Mark it in your weekly stats as system downtime," he typed. "Call me tomorrow afternoon and we'll see if it's the servers."

Then he thought it would give him a good opportunity to go back to Park Forest over the weekend. Mike wrote his assistant he would be in Rockford Saturday and Sunday and shutdown his computer. He flipped off the lights off in his office and nodded a greeting to someone on the cleaning staff. Walking out to the lobby and down the stairs, he stepped outside to the parking lot.

Mike surveyed the parking lot. A moonless night, the sky was inky black with pinprick stars. There were two cars in the lot, more than likely the cleaners. A number of the overhead lights were out and the edges of the parking lot were lost to the darkness. He couldn't help but recall that this might have been how it was when Becky was taken.

From across the lot in a shadowy corner, Mike heard the faint thump thump thump and low bass tone of hip hop music. An engine started up and revved loudly. Mike started quickly across the lot for his car.

Tires squealed and the vehicle, with headlights off, roared out of the corner and crossed the parking lot at a rapid clip.

The thump thump thump grew louder. The shadowy car accelerated.

Mike glanced over. Something wasn't right about the car. It sped in his direction. He reached his car but fumbled digging the keys out of his pocket.

The thump thump thump got nearer, louder.

Mike felt around the asphalt searching for his keys. "Shit."

The car raced toward him across the lot. In the flash of an overhead light Mike saw a small blue coupe. His heart pounded in his chest. His fingers touched his key ring and he grabbed the keys and pressed the fob. He fumbled with the door handle. He realized he'd hit the lock button.

The headlights of the car flashed on bright and blinding Mike. He put his hand up to shield his eyes and tried to pull his phone from his pocket. Thump thump thump, the car looked as if it was going to broadside Mike's car, pinning him between. He thought he might have to vault to the top of his car to save his life.

A loud screech of tires, the smell of burnt rubber and the car turned sideways—sliding at Mike.

He leapt out of the way, darting around the trunk of his car. The coupe slid to a stop but inches from the side of Mike's car. The windows of the coupe were so dark Mike couldn't see anyone inside.

His keys in one hand, phone in the other, Mike held the phone up to the light of the coupe's headlights and tried to punch in 911. The coupe gunned its engine and lurched forward, toward Mike. He circled around his car, trying to keep it between him and the blue coupe. The coupe's tires squealed coming around the side of Mike's car. With all the engine noise and tires squealing and thump thump thump, Mike couldn't hear if he had reached 911 on the phone. He looked at the screen, he hadn't pressed SEND. The coupe revved and turned chasing Mike to the front of his car. He hit SEND, backing around his car.

"911," the female voice answered. "What is the nature of your emergency?"

"I'm in the Infobyte parking lot, in West Des Moines, and some maniac is trying to run me down," Mike breathlessly said.

"Run you down? How sir?"

Thump thump thump, the tires spun and smoke billowed around Mike.

"Can't you hear that?"

"I hear tires, sir. Is that the car?"

"Yes, hurry..."

"We have a patrol car in the area," she said. "Stay on the phone with me, sir."

The blue coupe wheeled and took off after Mike. He turned and ran toward the nearest light pole. The coupe accelerated and sped right on Mike's heels. He jumped to one side, but the car jerked after him. He reached the light pole and crouched behind the concrete base. The coupe braked loudly, then circled the light pole. Clouds of blue smoke engulfed Mike as he kept the concrete base between him and the coupe. Then slowly, pacing Mike, the coupe followed him round the light pole. This went two or three times.

Then, for no apparent reason, the coupe peeled off and tore across the parking lot It swerved out the exit and the thump thump thump sped off into the night.

Mike stood up, coughing and waving the blue smoke away from his face. He gagged on the stink of burnt rubber.

"Sir?" The 911 operator called from his phone. "Are you still there?"

"I'm here." Mike replied, taking a deep breath and trying to calm himself.

"Are you alright?"

"Yeah," he said. "Whoever that maniac was, he just drove off." Mike walked over to his car.

"Has the patrol car arrived yet?"

Mike glanced up and saw headlights coming slowly in the entrance. "I think they just got here." The car drove up through lingering clouds of blue tire smoke. It was West Des Moines police. "Yeah," Mike said. "They're here, operator. Thanks a lot." He clicked off the phone as the patrol car pulled up and two cops got out.

"You called 911?" One cop said.

"What's the trouble?" The second asked getting out from the driver's side.

"I got off work late and was walking to my car when another car raced across the lot. They tried to run me down."

One cop puckering up his face. "Phew, burnt tires. Is that from the car?" The second cop reported to dispatch on his shoulder microphone.

"Yeah," Mike said. "The car just kept coming after me."

"Any idea why they tried to run you down?" The second cop stepped around the front of the patrol car approaching Mike. When he moved he sounded like creaky leather.

Mike hesitated. "Nope, no idea," he said, shaking his head and looking away. He didn't want to go into it with the cops though he was certain it was the same blue coupe that met him at his house the previous night.

"Did you get the license number?"

"I don't think it had plates. I was running. I didn't have a chance to look."

"What about the make of the vehicle?"

"I didn't see any car emblem." Mike shook his head. "It was definitely a small Japanese coupe, blue, but I couldn't tell you what make."

"See who was driving?"

"The windows were dark. I couldn't see anyone in the car."

The second cop squatted down. "Look at these skid marks." He followed them around Mike's car. "Well, I'd say they were definitely after you."

"Can I get your name?" the other cop asked, taking out a small notebook from his breast pocket and clicking a pen.

"Sure. It's Smith, Michael Smith," he said, as the cop wrote it down. Without being asked he recited his address in West Des Moines. This got the attention of the second cop who had been following the trail of the skid marks.

"Excuse me," he said, hesitantly. "Aren't you the Mike Smith whose wife was murdered about six months ago?"

Mike drew back, silently regarding the cop. "Yeah," he answered slowly. "Why?"

"I was on the team that went out to Jordan Creek where they found the body," he said. "This old fart and his retard grandson were out hunting for bugs to eat, or something like that." He turned to his partner. "Man, Bill, you should have seen what they did to this chick."

Bill, his eyes wide in horror, held his hand up. "Not the place," he hissed under his breath.

"They screwed this gal up and down, in every hole, and then they hacked her up."

"Dan!"

Mike gaped, horrified.

"Arms, legs, hands scattered it all over the creek. They even cut out her pussy. But...what was weird was they carved cuss words—and a big anarchist star on her back."

Bill pushed his partner back toward the patrol car. "That's enough, Dan! It's the guy's wife." He went back over to Mike. "I'm really sorry about that. My partner doesn't know when to shut up sometimes."

"Are you done with me?"

"Yeah, I think we got what we needed."

The other cop, Dan, squinted up at the light poles. "Ya know," he pointed. "There's a surveillance camera on that light. We could come back tomorrow and pull the tapes and see if we can get a plate or make of the car."

The other cop walked Mike to his car. "What's that on your windshield?" A piece of paper tucked under the windshield wiper flapped in a slight breeze. Mike pulled it out and read: "You didn't lisen, *Senor Cabron*. Led it go." It was written in black marker, scrawling thick across the page.

"Lisen? Do they mean listen? Listen to what, Mr. Smith?"

Mike wadded up the note and tossed it into his car. "That has nothing to do whoever tried to run me over."

"No?" The cop looked at him skeptically.

"This is work related. It's nothing," Mike said dismissively, waving. "We had a meeting this afternoon. You know, delicate egos."

The cop stood silent, staring at Mike.

He shuffled about, uncomfortable.

"You want to swear out a complaint?" Hands on his hips, the cop finally asked.

"No," Mike replied with a shrug. "Maybe it was just some kids fooling around."

He looked at Mike.

"Yeah," Mike added. "Just some kids I guess." He opened the driver's side door. "Well, thanks for coming out. I think I'm alright now."

"We're going to have to write up the call. If you remember any other details be sure to let us know."

"Oh, I will," Mike assured him. "Thanks again."

"Good night Mr. Smith," the cop said, pocketing his notebook and returning to the patrol car.

Mike sat behind the wheel and slammed the door. He took a deep breath, still stunned by the cop talking about Becky's body. Glad to be rid of them before their questions got too close, Mike warmed up his car and watched the patrol car wheel slowly around the lot and ease out the exit.

9

"Meet me at the clock tower at Park Forest Plaza 7pm-Grace," read the text on his phone.

Mike drove east on I-80 just outside of Davenport. He didn't recognize the number; it wasn't Grace's. He couldn't text back, not while driving, but would at the next gas stop. He wouldn't be able to go to the Rockford Call Center and make the 5pm meeting with Grace. Rockford would have to wait.

He had been driving I-80 from Des Moines to Illinois so frequently that he knew almost every rut and rock in the road. He hadn't been to Park Forest since the Rich High reunion in June. That was at night and he didn't stay. He took the same route I-80 to Highway 57 that he took to Monee when he went to see Donnie. He had bypassed Park Forest then, but this time he would be returning to the suburb and neighborhood where he grew up.

When he was young Sauk Trail was a two lane road that went through Park Forest. Sauk Trail and Western Avenue were the main arteries east to west and north to Chicago. Mike turned at the Sauk Trail exit off Highway 57 that led to Park Forest. The Park Forest where Mike grew up still looked the model of suburbia sprouted from cornfields in the late 1940s. It offered affordably priced homes of a generally similar ranch style design with three bedrooms and two baths on a concrete slab, with good-sized lots. The street corners were round, schools and shopping centers were built close by, almost within a few blocks. For an area of specific geography and population an elementary school was built. Then a middle school was built as the 2.5 kids grew to middle school age. It was a planned in specific detail community and governed conservatively. That always bothered Mike—the suburban monoculture. Once he had seen other parts of the world he realized it was not the homogenized reality of Park Forest. Park Forest was a lie on the face of a diverse world. Mostly Mike remembered Park Forest as kids, kids on bikes, kids in cliques, kids at Friday school dances, kids at the Saturday matinee at the Holiday Theater, kids close in age groups, kids in similar clubs and sports, and kids growing up together apace.

Newer subdivisions with more modern two story homes dotted the road into Park Forest. The deeper into Park Forest he got the more visible were the older ranch style homes. He turned onto Blackhawk Drive, his old street and noted little had changed as he drove closer to his block and the house across the street from Blackhawk Elementary and Blackhawk Middle School. There on the right, the house he grew up in. He slowed and looked. It was a different color with more trees and hedges and one tall oak with a large leafy canopy in the front yard. This was the same house hiding under a new coat of paint. Seeing where he grew up didn't move him as much as he thought it would. There was no emotional connection and he had a difficult time picturing himself there. He drove down the slight decline of Blackhawk Drive. "This used to be a big hill when I was younger," Mike thought.

On the opposite side of the street were the models of the prairie school of design, the rectangular red brick Blackhawk Elementary and behind it the campus of red brick rectangular Blackhawk Middle School. The open field where all summer Mike played pickup baseball, still showed rutted base paths. Donnie and Gary played in those hot summer days. They, and baseball, were innocent then. Decker hardly ever came out to play.

This wasn't the sprawling and big town he recalled as a child. As if from memory at the bottom of Blackhawk

Drive, he turned left on Orchard Street as he had done countless times as a boy on his bicycle riding to Little League games or the Aqua Center or the shopping center. He passed the small park where every winter the town would flood a large area turning it into an ice rink. He and Grace had ice skating dates and sometimes her kid sister Chastity would tag along.

Mike checked his watch. He had time. What did Grace want to talk to him about?

A couple of blocks and Mike rolled to the intersection of what had been the large parking lot of the Park Forest Plaza. But it had changed, with grassy areas, hedges and saplings. Nothing looked the same. One of the first outdoor malls in the country, with Jewel, Sears and Goldblatt's stores as anchors, the plaza had been the model for suburbs of the future. It didn't seem much of a mall now. A sign read Park Forest Village Center. The shopping center was where kids would go on Saturdays to see a movie, get penny candy at the white-tile Karmel Korn shop, or buy the latest plastic car or airplane model at the hobby shop. As kids grew to teenagers the shopping center became the meeting place. They would walk around in groups looking at other kids, seeing who and being seen themselves. Mike parked in a small lot and walked up to a two story building and what he remembered to be the Marshall Fields, a very upscale department store way back then.

Park Forest Plaza had been designed like a wheel, with spokes off a central open area, the hub which Mike walked into. He passed some upscale storefronts. Graffiti tags were painted on concrete walls, but for the most part it was like a village common with walkways and manicured lawns. Over to his right used to be Goldblatt's, a Chicago area discount department store. That was gone. The sign with a leasing office and phone number in the display window used to be where Rothchild's, a clothing store that his mother would take him to for school clothes every August. There was a Mexican restaurant, pizza take-out and Indian restaurant. Across the open area was still the Holiday Theater where just about every Saturday afternoon he and his pals would go to see the latest science fiction or western movie. When he was older he would take a girl to the

Holiday and sit in the back row of the balcony to make out. This was now a six screen multiplex.

Decker Real Estate logo and phone number, with Rod's grinning face, graced every bus stop bench.

The whitewashed brick clock tower used to dominate this open area. When just a boy, Mike thought the triangular tower rose 100 feet tall; although, in reality, it was a third the height. He recalled seeing presidential candidates at pre-election rallies speaking in front of the clock tower. Park Forest honored his Rich High baseball team as it prepared for the state regional with a pep rally at the base of the clock tower. This was the symbol of Park Forest, but the clock tower was gone.

A lonely place now, with few shoppers and others coming for a quick bite to eat. It might not be a good idea to be here after dark.

He looked at his phone. Grace wasn't there. Why would she say to meet at the clock tower? Did it have something to do with where Grace and Chastity were abducted? If that were true, Mike didn't know why she would ever want to come back here again.

"Looking for the old clock tower?" a voice spoke from behind Mike. "Shitty Smitty, Heh...heh...heh."

Mike spun around and saw Decker stepping out from under the shadow of a red roofed building. He was dressed in an expensive three piece black pinstripe suit and wore dark wraparound sunglasses.

"Decker?" Mike replied. "What are you doing here?"

"Shopping."

"Really? Shopping? Not too many places here to browse."

"I was misled," Decker replied with a sneer. There was a hard arrogance to his tone. "They tore the clock tower down in 1987. Shame, isn't it? But you didn't know that. You were out traveling the world. So why are you here?"

"I had a hankering for a curry and Kingfisher."

"Cut the crap," said a small old man in a long navy blue wool coat. "It's been a long time, Mr. Mike Smith." He walked with a halt and out from behind Decker.

"You remember my Pop."

Mike straightened up, surprised. "Mr. Decker?" He hesitantly held out his hand.

"Stick it back in your pocket, Smith," the old man snarled. "You know who I am."

"Yeah, Sam Decker. Rod's poppa?"

Sam Decker audibly sighed. "Don't be so goddamn cute. You were always smarter than that."

"I know you moved up from superintendent. "You a principal now? Maybe a substitute teacher?" His sarcasm had an effect.

"Watch your mouth," Decker angrily interjected. "Pop's THE Illinois state school superintendent," he said poking a finger in Mike's face.

"He knows, son," the old man said, holding a hand up.

Mike swatted Rod's finger away. "What do you want with me?"

"I've been told you've been nosing around, asking questions and making accusations about some petty things. These things are from a long time ago. Things that never happened."

Mike said nothing, his head cocked to the side regarding the old man with narrow eyes.

Old man Decker again sighed, pinching his nose and glancing away as if annoyed. "Have it your way, Smith." He stepped forward, in front of his taller son. He seemed tiny, spindly and all but swallowed up by the navy blue coat. His narrow face was pale, with long creases down either cheek. A slight breeze ruffled long white strands of hair barely covering his brown freckled scalp. He spoke with a thin, reedy voice. "I am not going to let you tarnish the memory, nor belittle the accomplishments, of the '79 baseball team."

Mike squared his head and peered down at the smaller man. "Is that what you think this is all about? The old team?"

"Isn't it, Smith?"

Mike paused, staring into the old man's dull grey eyes.

"If this is to uphold the honor of some dirty girl, I might laugh myself to death."

"No, it isn't," Mike replied. "It's to keep the animals separate from the human beings."

"Let me offer you some advice. Stop asking questions. That was so very sad about your little wife's murder. You need to get over it. Now get back to your work and stop troubling yourself and bothering others with silly made up stories from long ago," he said as he turned.

"Or what?" Mike said.

"Oh don't be melodramatic," the old man replied as he limped away. "There doesn't need to be or what—unless you want it. Come on, son."

Rod Decker followed, then turned about. "She's not coming, Shitty."

"Yeah?"

"I mean—she's not coming, ever," Decker said, slowly walking backward. "Like the clock tower, like the plaza, like Park Forest when we were kids, she's not here anymore."

"What do you mean?" Mike started after them. "If you did anything to her...."

"Nobody did nothing to anybody, Smitty, Heh...heh...heh." Decker called, rounding the corner of a building just behind his father. "That's the point."

Mike ran after Decker, but stopped short when he recognized the heavyset black man and small Hispanic man standing at the corner blocking Mike. "I know where you live," he yelled after Decker and his dad. "I know what you did. You, Gary and Donnie...and..." Mike jabbed his finger in the air at the old man climbing into the back seat of a black Cadillac Seville. "...and you, Sam Decker. You'll pay; I'll make sure of it."

Mike backed away from the two men, taking out his phone. He wheeled and keyed in Grace's phone number. He jogged through the village center back to his car. Grace's line rang, and rang twice. "Pick up," he breathed. "Please...pick up.

"Michael." It was Grace.

"Grace...don't hang up," he said quickly, breathing hard.

"You have to stop calling. I told you I don't want to talk to you."

"Are you okay?"

"Yes?" There was a question in Grace's voice. "Why?"

"Nobody called you?" Mike stopped, panting. "Or..." he hesitated. "Or...anything?"

"No," She sounded confused. "Just you Michael and you have to stop. I told you I am not going to tell you anything about..." Grace abruptly stopped. "We don't have anything to talk about, Michael."

He got to his car and dug in his pocket for his keys. "I know, Grace. I don't think you need to tell me anything." He pressed the button on his key fob and unlocked his car. "I think I know what happened."

Mike sat in his car and closed the door. Dusk scrubbed the blue sky to grey. The seatbelt bell sounded over and over. Tension lifted off his shoulders and he let out a long breath. "Grace, it's not about you or your sister anymore. And I am so sorry about Chastity. I found out last week...from Gary Watson."

Grace said nothing.

"Okay, don't talk. But please listen. I bet you and your sister were not the only girls Decker, his dad, Gary and Donnie abducted and raped."

Grace remained silent. But she hadn't hung up.

"I think I know what happened now and I'm going to expose them."

A few moments passed.

"Michael," Grace finally broke the silence, replying slowly, calculating each word. "All that is in the past. It's over. It's done. It only comes back as a bad dream...and on Chastity's birthday. Sometimes when I hear a certain word, I can't help being afraid. I jump when a car pulls up next to me. But I survived. I have a good life with Jeff. I have a family and loving children. Jeff doesn't know anything about it. My kids don't know about it. I'm funny mom because I won't go out alone at night. They laugh when I make sure every door is locked. I will never tell them. I can't go back there....I won't go back there."

"Grace," Mike quietly said. "I won't take you back there. I won't bother you anymore."

"Are you okay?"

"I am. I am," he replied. "I can't get my Becky back, but I can punish the bastards that did this terrible thing to you and Chastity. It's like I've been throwing punches in a dark room and hoping my fists find a target. I feel like I am righting something that's terribly wrong, an old and evil wrong."

"Be careful Michael. These aren't hollow men you're going after."

"I will," he calmly said. "I know what I am doing."

Grace hung up.

10

Lights burned inside the single story square brick building of the Park Forest Daily. It was after 9 o'clock. Relieved to see the lights, Mike pulled into the parking lot. He put his car into park and shut off the ignition. It didn't matter if his classmate Bill More was at the office, he had to get inside the Daily's office.

From his overnight bag in the backseat, Mike fished out the blood-stained notebook. Dog-eared corners, dirt and ink smudged some pages from frequent leafing. Mike flipped to an open page and started to jot notes from his encounter with the Deckers, son and father. The light from an overhead florescent lamp made the page glow yellow. He jotted down what had happened at the meeting and what they said. Circumstantial at best, but why had Decker warned him to stop nosing around and asking questions.

Mike had hit it, the four Donnie Inge, Gary Watson, Rod Decker and his father, Sam Decker, had abducted and repeatedly raped Grace and her sister Chastity. In brackets, Mike noted the call to Grace with her comments about 'the past being the past'. The crime had been committed.

Confirmation could be drawn from Sam Decker's reaction and veiled threats. Should he go to the police? There was no physical evidence. He bet Grace would refuse to testify. It'd be his accusations against Decker's denials. Mike closed the notebook and slipped it into the side pocket of his jacket.

He pulled on the handle in the dark alcove entrance of the Daily. The doors were locked. Through tinted windows he could see a few people at desks working on computers in the office. Mike tapped the glass with his key. An elderly woman with wiry white hair in a blue and orange Bears t-shirt approached. She twisted the latch, opening the door a few inches.

"I'm sorry, we're closed."

"I know," Mike hurriedly said. "I have something for Bill More, the senior editor. Can I give it to you?

"What's it regarding?"

"It's personal. We went to Rich High together."

"No problem," she said, jerking the door open. Mike sidestepped in. "He's working late tonight." There was a long counter across the front of the room and overhead, oversized sign dividing Sales, Classified Ads on one side; News, Features, Photo, Sports on the other. Musky smells filled the room, ozone, stale coffee and copier toner.

"Bill's the last on the left," she pointed to the back and a small office with the lights on. "I'll let him know you're here," she said with a smile. "HEY BILL," she bellowed across the newsroom, startling no one. "Some guy's here to see you."

The newsroom computers resembled a garage sale with electronics from the late nineties through early 2000s. A few new screens were interspersed with PC towers and occasional clunky laptops, the hand-me-downs for the suburban stepchild of the Tribune.

Bill popped his head up from behind a computer screen at his desk.

"Thanks," Mike quietly said to the woman.

"You betcha."

Bill recognized Mike coming down the aisle between desks and broke into a wide grin. "Mike," he said. "It's good to see you."

"I didn't think I'd find you here." They shook hands quickly over Bill's cluttered desk.

"Coffee?" Bill asked. "Pop? I can't offer you anything stronger."

"What the heck kind of newspaper man are you. Don't you have a bottle of whiskey tucked under files in the bottom drawer of your desk? It's okay, I'm good." Mike grinned, settling on a short worn couch to the left of Bill's desk. "Why are you working late anyway. I thought you were the boss?"

Bill settled back in his creaking desk chair, smiling. "Being the boss at a newspaper nowadays doesn't offer many perks. I write news, editorials and even some sports. I stand in for the publisher at Chamber of Commerce luncheons, ribbon cutting new roads and I have posed with a shovelful of dirt at the future site of an office building. Hey, I even sell a few ads. Being senior editor means I am factotum."

"Factotum? What does that pay?"

"A handful of denarii."

Bill eschewed filing for piling as there were stacks of papers, folders, magazines and books heaped on any shelf space available. The framed pictures on the wall were cock-eyed or tilted like Bill's diploma from Northwestern. Only the large color photo of his red haired Edie, posing like a fashion model, hung straight and true. Styrofoam coffee cups, fast food bags and plastic soft drink bottles overflowed from the trash can next to his desk.

"Boss?" A tall thin middle-aged man in faded red The Varsity-Atlanta t-shirt and grey and red flannel shirt leaned in the doorway. "I'm about to head out."

"Come on in and introduce yourself," Bill said with a wave. The lanky man cautiously entered the office. "This is Mike Smith, third baseman on Rich High's '79 baseball team." Bill added as an aside to Mike. "Dig this."

"I'm Richard, Rich, Richie don't fucking call me Dick...Rice." Out stretched Rich's bony hand. Mike glanced at Bill. They chuckled. Rich smiled. Rugged looking, with a growth of stubble on his long face, Rich's short pepper black hair was messy and sprinkled with silver. He bore a more than passing resemblance to Steve McQueen. Rich shook Mike's hand and gave him an engaging smile.

"Isn't that the best intro you've ever heard?" Bill said.

"You sound like Dick 'don't call me Richie' Allen from the Sox. How long you been a sports writer?"

"Sports?" Rich exclaimed. "Do I look like I smoke pot?"

"I just thought since..." Mike knew Rich was ribbing him.

"I'm a news man," Rich assured him.

"Oh, what do news men smoke then?"

Bill and Rich broke up laughing.

"I like this guy, Bill," he said, then excused himself with a wave. "Nice meeting you, Mike."

"Same here, Rich"

"That story's in your edit queue. See you in the morning, boss."

"Alright Rich," Bill said as they settled back into their seats. "Helluva writer. Old school."

"So why are you working so late tonight?" Mike asked.

"Editing copy for our online edition," Bill responded. "I don't know what the heck J schools are teaching these days, but some of the stuff I see would have you rolling on the floor in hysterics."

"Really? Try me? I need a laugh."

"I've seen R O D iron, rod iron, for wrought iron more than a couple times." He warmed to the topic. "An intern turned in a story saying a political candidate had *passed mustard*. A copy editor caught that and handed it back with a sticky note that read you must mean *pass muster* because if he is passing mustard he needs to see a doctor." Bill let out a loud laugh to Mike's toothy grin.

"Another reporter covering a politician wrote he wrestled with the issue, saying it was his *cross-eyed bear*. I asked her, 'are you sure he said cross-eyed bear and not CROSS I BEAR? Poor kid didn't have a clue."

"Oh, couple years ago we had a news guy sub for the sports editor one time when UCLA and USC played a big football game. The game ran late and the next day the banner headline." Bill paused for effect. "Sports section-- top of the page," he spread his hands wide. "Read: USC

Beats the Trojans." He bounced in glee as if seeing the gaffe for the first time. "I think that showed up on the inside back page of the Columbia Journalism Review."

Mike shook his head as much amused as in disbelief. He needed to let loose.

"But my favorite," Bill enthused, moving forward in his chair. "My absolute all-time favorite was a line a reporter wrote in a story about people leaving their pets in cars on hot summer days with the windows rolled up." He lowered his voice, feigning seriousness. "He wrote: The death rate was 100 percent for those fatally struck."

Eyebrows arched, Bill mugged at Mike. It took Mike a couple of seconds to comprehend the line.

"C'mon," Bill exclaimed. "That's funny."

"Yeah, that's a good one."

"So tell me," Bill asked, changing the subject. "What brings you out to Park Forest?"

"We have VoIP issues at the Rockford Call Center," Mike said, looking away, knowing he wasn't sounding convincing.

"Rockford? Not one of your sub-continent destinations. We're kind of out-of-the-way."

"Ah, maybe a little bit," Mike shrugged.

"Well, whatever the reason, it's great to see you again. I was glad we reconnected at the reunion and I'm glad you stopped by." Bill fell silent. "You hung out with the jocks and the A group in high school, but were always a regular guy. I remember a time in gym class when the bullies targeted me for a prank and you stepped in and..."

"Aw, c'mon," Mike interrupted, holding his hand up. "We all survived high school...somehow."

"Okay, you're embarrassed." He paused. "Say listen," he then added. "I'll be done here in about 10 or 15 minutes. Let me give Edie a call. She can meet us at the Embers Tap Room and we can have some burgers, beers and a few laughs."

"Sounds great, but I really should be heading up to Rockford."

"It's late, but suit yourself."

"I do have a question for you, though," Mike asked.

"Shoot."

"Does Decker's old man still have a house down in Thorn Creek?"

"Ah...yeah." Showing surprise, Bill slowly replied. "He's got a nice house down there. And the old man's in town too. He's getting some kind of award—The Bratva Humanitarian Lifetime Achievement award from a Russian philanthropic group or something like that. It's at the convention center tomorrow. The guy's really tight with Chicago Russians. He's become real powerful in the state legislature. Why do you want to know?"

"Thought I might drop by," Mike said matter-of-factly.

"Rod Decker made my life hell in high school," Bill said in a disgusted tone. "Now he's a shyster real estate mogul who buys about half the pages in the Daily every Sunday. The old man gave me the creeps. He was always leering at the girls."

"He was a supporter of the baseball team and I thought I would pay my respects."

"A lot of people die around that guy. Well, Bob Picolo, your baseball coach. A hunting accident they called it."

"I heard about that. I should get going, Bill." Mike half rose from the couch. He surreptitiously lifted the notebook from his jacket pocket and let it fall. "It was good to see you. Give my best to Edie."

"I certainly will, Mike." They shook hands. "You have to come out to the house for a barbeque. You can regale me with tales of your travels around the world."

"That's a deal," Mike said at the office door. "Remind me to tell you about the Air India flight I took from Delhi to Frankfurt, Germany We left Indira Ghandi International with 200 souls and landed one shy."

"I'm intrigued," Bill said with a beaming smile. "Great tease for a story."

The older lady met Mike at the door, letting him out.

"Thanks," Mike said.

"Night," she replied.

11

Mike knew the location of Decker's Thorn Creek house, remembering the many baseball team parties and gatherings with boosters in his junior varsity and varsity seasons. He also recalled the rumors of other parties, with beer, drugs and girls. The girls weren't girlfriends or high school-aged girls. Some of the girls, it was said, were hookers imported from Chicago. Mike wasn't invited to these parties.

He drove down the dark suburban street. Night had fallen, picture windows glowed yellow from living room lights in houses outlined by darkness. Snug and cozy, doors locked against the outside world. A man walked his dog along the sidewalk. Mike turned off Monee Road onto a street light lit, tree-lined lane. Houses were invisible behind trees and fences, set way back from the road and behind locked gates.

Low watt bulbs gleamed on either side of the tall wrought iron gate at the entrance to Decker's property. Strangely, the gate was wide open.

Old man Decker's house was ritzy decades ago and it was still high-class. A mid-century, quasi-Frank Lloyd Wright designed prairie ranch. The house had lots of large glass windows in each of its square sections. Illuminated by landscape lighting, it was a house of simple geometry and horizontal line, with a long middle structure of rough-hewn brown wood and two flanking structures of flagstone. The main living area had an overhang and balcony that seemed to hover above Thorn Creek. With its shallow shake roof and suppressed chimney the house all but blended into the surrounding woodsy hillside.

Mike eased up the curving blacktop drive. He could see cars in a bay to the side. There was the blue coupe that was parked in front of his house and nearly ran him down in the office parking lot. Next to the coupe was a black Cadillac Seville and van. Mike stopped his car, turned off the lights and got out. His stomach had the jitters. "I survived," he remembered Grace saying. But your sister did not, Mike thought.

He walked around the front of his car. A figure came out of the darkness.

"We bean 'spectin' jew, *Cabron*," said the short Hispanic, flashing a twisted grin.

"Have you?"

"Ja, man. De old man he say you show up," he walked alongside Mike. "De old man, he one smart dude."

"The old man is a criminal, a rapist."

The Hispanic laughed. "He a smart rapist, *Cabron*." He opened the heavy wood front door for Mike. "He no never got caught."

Mike stepped up and over the threshold, into the house. Lights burned bright inside. The open floor plan of the living room featured floor-to-ceiling windows that dominated the far half of the room. The walls were painted off-white with recessed lighting. Cherry wood floors with plush white carpeting covered an area between two, facing fifties-style, modern white leather couches. A gas fire roared in a wide flagstone fireplace. Rod Decker sat at the far end of one couch, a beer in hand. The old man was in a tall straight-back wooden chair to the side of the hearth. Dwarfed by the high chair back the old man looked the picture of age and frailty.

A door ajar to a side room caught Mike's attention. Flickering grey blue light shone through the door.

"Looky what I find," the Hispanic said, giving Mike a shove into the middle of the room.

"*Gracias*, Javier," the old man said, then turned to his son. "I told you he would come around."

Decker raised his beer bottle to his dad. "Never should've doubted you, Pop."

"So how much?" The old man asked in his thin voice.

"How much what?" Mike replied. Muted noises like screams came from inside the side room.

"Don't you fucking waste my time, Smith. Money. Money." The old man hissed. "How much fucking money do you want to shut up and go away?"

"I don't want money."

"Shitty Smitty," Decker said wearily. "You're not being smart."

"I want you to pay for raping Grace and her sister Chastity," Mike demanded. "And I want to know when."

"Grace?" The old man glanced to his son. "Who the fuck is this Grace and her bitch sister?"

"Grace and her younger sister Chastity, you don't remember." Rod explained.

"Who?" The old man was getting irritated. "Who?"

Decker motioned with his hands to calm his father then turned to Mike. "He doesn't know, Shitty. Heh...heh...heh. We've had our way with just about every little piece of pussy in this town." Rod flashed a malicious smile.

"I don't know any Grace or Chastity," the old man muttered. "There are few uses for women, cook, clean, fetch and fuck. They're all sluts and whores. They all want it. Fuck me, they say. The little cunts beg for it. Rape? Men are the masters—that's not rape."

"Aren't you the enlightened educator."

"Let me tell you, sonny. Men only want three things in life: money, pussy and power."

Decker grinned at his dad, saying to Mike. "I'll tell you when we did it, Shitty," he smirked. "The night before the regionals. That's right...the night before she dumped you. Oh, that was a night," he mocked. "We grabbed them at the shopping center and took them to a house and we fucked them silly, Heh...heh...heh. Drinking and screwing all night long. I don't know how the fuck we got to that game." Decker laughed.

"You son of a bitch," Mike lunged for Decker, but Javier grabbed him from behind.

"Hey, what's going on out here?" Out from the dark room came Donnie, Javier's large black partner and Gary.

"Playing hearts tonight, Gary?" Mike said. Gary wouldn't make eye contact. "Did you pray today?"

That got Gary's attention. His face flushed. "You shut up."

"Milly's going to find out about you."

Donnie swaggered up to Mike. His face still showed bruises, scrapes and black below his eyes from Mike's beating. "Keep hold of him," he said. "I need to settle something." Donnie punched Mike in the belly. Then he upper cut Mike on the chin. He bit his lip, stood up and glared back at Donnie. "I still won't let you suck my dick," Mike growled spitting blood in Donnie's face.

"That's enough," Decker yelled, standing.

"Let him see the videos of his precious little bitches," the old man said. "Then get rid of him."

Rod half turned, looking back at his father. "Rid of him?"

"Do you want to go to Springfield or to Joliet?" Sam Decker said with some exasperation. "May I remind you we have guests arriving later."

"Going to kidnap some young girls?" Mike managed to groan out.

The old man threw his head back and laughed with a sound like a cackle. "We no longer enjoy our little hunt. Russian friends have become very accommodating with some tasty treats to our liking." Sam Decker waved his hand. "Go away and see your videos."

"Videos?"

"Yeah, videos," Decker said with a nasty chuckle. "Bring him," he motioned for Javier to bring him into the room. They went in and turned on the lights.

Bill rubbed his eyes and pressed the save icon on the computer screen for the last news story on his computer. He glanced at his watch, editing had taken longer than the 10 or 15 minutes he told Mike it would. He logged off the network, rose and stretched. He took his coat off the chair back and slipped it on. He thought about seeing Mike, recalling how glad he was he stopped by to see him. "Got to be tough losing your wife that way," he said to himself. "Okay, I am out of here," he added, dropping his phone into his pocket. From habit, he paused at the door with a hand on the light switch surveying the office in case he'd left anything. Something on the couch caught Bill's eye. He went over and picked it up. It was a well-worn, stained notebook he didn't recognize. He opened to the first page.

"Donnie tells me Grace and her sister Chastity were taken from the shopping center and gang raped. I'm stunned. But who did this..."

Rough hands manhandled Mike. He fought as they dragged him into the side room. Intense white light blinded him. He held his hand up to his eyes and squinting could make out figures sitting and standing around the room, looking at a big screen with naked figures writhing around on a bed. A girl screamed. A child sobbed. Men laughed.

Then the ceiling fell in. That's what Mike thought as he came back to consciousness. He struggled to his hands and knees from the floor.

"What the..." he breathed, shaking his head.

Stars exploded in his eyes as something hit him hard in the back of the head. His ears rang and pain pounded. He collapsed to his belly.

A boot smashed into his face and he rolled to the side. Blood spewed from his nose and filled his mouth. He thought he had rocks in his mouth. No, those weren't rocks. His front teeth, upper and lower, had been shattered.

Mike coughed and spat blood with pieces of teeth.

A high pitched voice talked fast, frantic in what seemed another language.

Another boot cracked him on the side of his head. He lay flat, trying to get up.

"He always had good hands," a man's voice said. "Break'em."

The fat end of a wood baseball bat slammed down on the back of his hand.

Pain shot up Mike's arm. He let out a cry.

From all over boots and bats landed blows again and again up and down his rib cage.

Blackness, as if a curtain rung down.

Mike woke when grabbed and pulled from the floor and out the door.

Again it turned black.

Voices filtered through darkness as he went in and out of consciousness. He tumbled into the back of a van. A door slid and slammed. The engine started.

It seemed minutes, but then the door opened. Hands hauled Mike out of the van by his feet. Cold air stung his battered face. He coughed. His ribs hurt with each breath. He was outside and it was night. Carried from the van, he heard cars and trucks passing nearby. Held up under his arms, Mike tried to raise his head to shout for help, but couldn't move.

The dried snot and clotted blood clogged his nose. Mike's breath came in ragged gasps through his mouth. Someone jerked his head back and forced his mouth open. Liquor poured down his throat and burned the inside of his mouth. He spit up and sputtered. They laughed around him.

"Don't waste the good stuff."

A small figure walked up and stood in silhouette against car headlights.

"You were always too smart for your own good." The hard slap knocked Mike's head sideways. They carried him to a car, his car he realized, and pushed him into the driver's seat.

"I can get away," he thought.

Someone strapped him in tight with the seat belt. He watched through unfocused eyes as an arm reached across and started the car. The open door warning bell sounded over and over. The engine revved up. Another arm put a rubber band over the steering wheel and looped the end over the seat lever.

"Steering wheel's set." A heavily accented voice said.

"Set cruise control," another voice added.

Though groggy, Mike knew the voice.

"Ready?"

"Yeah," someone yelled over the engine noise. "Flip it into drive."

The car lurched forward and both doors slammed. Accelerating, Mike's head snapped back. He was going fast down the hill on a single lane. Tiny lights ahead moved across the windshield. He felt elated a moment--he had escaped. A beeping noise sounded on his phone. Becky?

Big round lights closed—growing brighter as he raced to the bottom of the lane. He sped into a swarm of lights. A red sign flashed past: Wrong Way. He tried to move his feet—to hit the brake. He couldn't move. A sound like a train horn blared loud and louder, bearing down on him. White light flooded the inside of the car. Tires squealed....

Bill looked up from the page, his mouth agape. "Oh my god," he breathed. "This is Mike's notebook." He recollected Grace House had been Mike's girlfriend in high school. Bill went back to his desk and sat, leafing through the notebook. He took out his phone.

"Edie," he said, distracted. "I'm sorry, dear, but something has come up and I'll be a little late."

"You okay, Bill?" Edie asked. "You don't sound right."

"I'm okay. I'm just reading something disturbing."

Bill clicked off from Edie and turned to the inside front cover of the notebook. A phone number with a West Des Moines area code was written in the corner. After three rings, Mike's message came on.

"Mike, it's me, Bill. You left your notebook in my office," he said. "I didn't know it was yours at first, please forgive me but I looked inside for a name and read some of the stuff in the notebook." He took a deep breath. "Mike, what is this all about? This is pretty explosive stuff. I mean, you're implicating some powerful people with crimes like kidnap and rape. Look, call me. I want to talk to you about this."

Bill closed the notebook and held it in both hands, thoughtfully looking at it. He took out his keys and opened a bottom drawer of his desk. He put the notebook in the drawer and locked it.

12

Balancing a tall cup of coffee from the drive-thru coffee kiosk, tucking copies of the Tribune and Sun-Times under his other arm, picking his brief case off the car seat and putting it on the car roof, Bill started his work day with a kick to close the driver's side door of his car. He scrambled across the parking lot of the Park Forest Daily with his awkward and shifting load. Working late the night before always made for a bad morning of being late and forgetful. But more than that—what Bill had read in Mike's notebook gave him a sleepless night of tossing and turning.

"Let me get that for you, boss," Rich said jogging up.

"Thanks, Rich," Bill said surprised. "What the heck are you doing here this early?" he added passing through the door.

The large newsroom hummed with chatter, clatter and bustle from reporters, sales staff on the telephone and people moving about, while others typed on keyboards.

Rich trailed behind Bill as they went down the aisle to Bill's office. "Have you read the Trib yet?" he asked.

"No," Bill replied, handing Rich his coffee cup to hold as he sorted through a key ring and then unlocked his office door. "I haven't had a chance yet. What's up?"

"Bill? I need to talk to you," a reporter called from a desk in the middle of the newsroom. Bill nodded.

Flipping on the overhead lights Bill crossed to his desk as Rich flopped on the short couch.

"That guy you introduced me to last night?" Rich started.

"Who? Mike?" Bill interrupted. Standing behind his desk, he dropped his brief case and then the folded newspapers onto his desk and took off his jacket. "Why?"

Rich rubbed his chin, looking left and right, but not at Bill. "Yeah. You need to read the South Suburban section of the Trib."

"You seem spooked," Bill said with a quizzical look. He picked through the folded newspapers and plucked the South Suburban section of the Tribune.

"Page two, column one...bottom."

Bill spread the Tribune out on his desk and leaned over, turning to page two. The page was full of weather and jumps from page one, section two.

"It's too damn early for a mystery, Rich," Bill complained, scanning the page. "What am I looking for?"

Rich jumped from the couch and went to the side of the desk and tapped his finger on a short, one column three-inch story with a three-deck headline: Drunk Driver, Causes I-80, Fatal Pile Up.

"An out-of-state man, possibly intoxicated, caused a truck and three-car pileup when he mistook the exit ramp as the entrance to I-80 Thursday night," Bill read aloud. "The driver, Michael C. Smith, 48, of West Des Moines, Iowa..." He stopped, glanced at Rich and slowly sat. "Shit, Rich. That's Mike." It took Bill a moment to compose himself and read on. "...entered oncoming traffic at a high rate of speed and collided with a semi-trailer truck. EMTs on the scene pronounced Smith dead." His mouth open, Bill looked away and shook his head.

"Keep reading," Rich said with a tight lipped expression. "I'm really sorry about your friend."

"Rich, this guy just lost his wife. I wonder if..."

"Read on," Rich urged.

"The accident occurred at Highway 45, South La Grange Road exit and eastbound I-80." Bill's voice lowered, thoughtful. "Police believe alcohol played a role in the driver mistaking the exit ramp for the interstate entrance. The driver's blood alcohol level was not released, pending autopsy. Empty liquor bottles were found among the charred wreckage of the vehicle."

"He didn't seem drunk to me when we were talking last night," Rich said. "It's too bad. He seemed like a real nice guy."

Bill said nothing, taking a deep breath and exhaling slowly through his nostrils, staring off into the newsroom.

"That's a really confusing cloverleaf down there," Rich continued, eying Bill. "I could see how someone from out of state might be disoriented."

"This doesn't make sense," Bill suddenly said, slamming his fist on the desk. He looked past Rich, thinking aloud, as if talking to himself. "He knows this area. He grew up in Park Forest. He told me he was going to Rockford. He wouldn't have taken Highway 45 to I-80. He'd have to drive all the way to 39 and then go north to Rockford. That's miles out of his way. He would've taken 284 to 290 at Elmhurst, then 90 at Schaumburg to Rockford. Something isn't right." Bill glanced down at his desk drawer. "He told me he was going to see old man Decker." He took his keys and unlocked the desk drawer, taking out the blood-stained notebook.

"Maybe he got lost," Rich said, watching Bill warily.

"Something smells," Bill said in a low, almost angry voice. "Something smells bad."

Rich stood up, hands on hips, studying Bill a moment. "What's up, Boss?"

Bill's slapped the notebook in his palm, his expression tight like anger, saying nothing for a while. "What're you working on?" he finally asked.

"Chicago Heights cops getting blow jobs in exchange for tearing up tickets to teenage girls...why?" Bill's demeanor told Rich something bigger than a one column, three-inch story of a traffic fatality percolated in his editor's brain.

Bill glanced at Mike's notebook. "This smells," he murmured, then turned to Rich. "Give that story to an intern," adding, "you're on this story."

"Story?" Rich questioned. "I know the guy was a friend, but it's just a drunk driving accident."

"No...it's not," Bill said. "Find out who's handling the accident Tinley Park or Orland Park PD. My guess is Tinley Park wouldn't want to touch it. They like to keep their stats clean. They probably handed it off to the state police. Call your contacts. I want all the details of the accident. And...you're going to see Sam Decker get an award this afternoon." Bill stood and started for the door.

"Old man Decker? The state Supe? That crook? I'm confused. What's Decker got to do with this?" Bewildered, Rich followed Bill. "What am I looking for here? Where's the story? It was just a traffic accident."

Bill stopped, turning on his heel. "When Mike Smith left here last night he was stone cold sober. He told me he was going out to see Sam Decker before driving to his call center in Rockford." Bill raised the notebook in his hand. "It's all in here, Rich" He handed Rich the notebook. "I want that back after you read it. Then you'll understand why this smells."

"Okay," Rich said slowly, studying the notebook in his hands. "Is that blood on the cover? What's in this?"

"Last thoughts of a man going after the bad guys—who knew his reward might be..." Bill paused.

"I'll make some calls and let you know what I find out." Rich sounded skeptical. "Where're you going?"

"I have to talk to my boss," Bill said, adding "and legal."

"Legal? Is this big?"

"Maybe."

"Snakes in the mailbox big?" Rich asked as Bill walked up the aisle between the desks.

"Ha! Bonus points for arcane newspaper knowledge," he replied over his shoulder.

13

Early morning sun bathed the sunroom in golden light and generous warmth. The large yellow circular sun had climbed the horizon and now touched the top casements of the screened windows. Grace sat motionless, the heat of the sun on her face, staring out to the backyard. Red, purple and white rose blossoms from the garden outside peeked just above the windowsills. She watched bees loop from flower to flower, pausing but moments. Birds sang as they swooped from tree to wire. This was her special time of the day in her favorite room of the house. She sat snug in the well molded cushions of a wicker chair. A cup of tea sweetened by honey, with soggy tea bag on the saucer, lay at hand. Diagonal cut cinnamon toast on a small plate sat between her outstretched arms on the circular wicker table. She noticed jelly stains, tea and coffee rings on the embroidered tablecloth and knew it needed changing. Wind chimes jingled on a slight breeze that gently rustled the leaves of the lemon tree in the backyard.

She had no taste for toast, nor tea.

The ripening yellow fruit of the lemon tree hung heavy from long limbs. The musk smell of mulch from the flowerbeds along the picket fence was in her nose.

Grace watched Mabel as she nosed around the yard. The spaniel mix was on the trail of something. She stopped, her long snout bobbing, catching a scent on the gentle wind.

A small black spider slowly inched its way up the wall to its web in the corner.

Lies are like spider's web made of sticky and non-sticky silk, she thought. The spider traverses the web on the non-sticky strands while an unwitting prey gets stuck on the sticky strands. Though sometimes even the spider, for all its elaborate weave, becomes ensnared in the web of its own design.

People are defined by their quiet moments. When they are alone and left within the drift of their thoughts, the truth of their happiness and satisfaction or unhappiness and dissatisfaction will out.

She didn't think of it at all, she often told herself. Then realized, she remembered every moment, every day. Her hand shook as she reached for her tea.

It came back in flashes. A car screeched to a stop next to them. Three boys jumped out and surrounded them. The gleaming knife poked in Grace's face. Chastity shrieked. A hand clapped over her mouth. They fought when they were grabbed and pulled into the back of the car. They were yelling. Grace knew them. The knife stung, stabbing her leg as a tear of blood rolled down her thigh. They pulled her hair and slipped a pillowcase over her head. "Chastity?"

Grace put the teacup to the saucer. It clattered on the china from her trembling.

The place smelled of alcohol, garbage, vomit and gasoline. Hands tore at her clothes, greedy for the flesh. Grace desperately clutched at the tearing fabric. Chastity screamed. Grace found her voice and yelled out "do anything you want to me, please leave my sister alone." They laughed, pushing her down onto a mattress. "Fuck her...fuck her...fuck her," they chanted. They pried her legs apart. The pain almost made her faint.

The toilet flushed inside the house. Grace knew Jeff was up.

Their pricks...their greasy dirty pricks. Over and over, one, another, then another, hours it seemed, though she may have passed out. "Leave her alone, Do anything you want to me." Light flashed to her right, then to her left, a click followed by a whirring sound. The pillowcase came loose and light burned her eyes, but she saw them. Rod, stinking of beer, grabbed her throat, squeezing the breath out of her lungs. "If you say one word you die. Your sister dies. Your mother and father die." Before she passed out Grace saw the little man standing behind the boys, watching with a twisted grin on his face. He had Chastity's hair bunched in his fists, holding her head down on him.

Jeff whistled in the kitchen. Grace knew he was pouring himself a cup of coffee. "Two sugars, milk," she thought.

Pitch dark when they were pushed out the car in the parking lot of the Park Forest Shopping Center. "Your mother will die. Your father will die if you say a word about this," Rod warned again. They drove off.

They clung to each other tightly and cried, huddled on the pavement of the parking lot. Caked blood smeared Grace's leg from the stab wound. "Don't tell anyone," Chastity said between sobs. "Don't tell mom or dad." They shivered together and tried to make their ripped clothing cover themselves. "Mom will think it was our fault and beat us," Grace said, sniffling. She hurt down there, bad. And she was bleeding.

"What about the police?" Chastity asked.

"Then everyone will know," Grace said as she helped Chastity up. Keeping to the shadows they slowly made their way home.

"Do you think they will really kill mom and dad?" Chastity sounded terrified. Grace had no answer.

And Michael, Grace thought, they were on his team. He'd find out. Bruised, bloodied and numb in heart, she wanted to shrink away from the world. Grace vowed to call Michael and break up. If Michael found out they would kill her mom and dad.

More than the fear, shame kept them silent. They never spoke of it again. No word of it ever passed between them. A look or a feeling was all that was ever communicated. Somehow it became known to a few. A leering glance in the school corridor, a comment from some girls in gym class, a snickering laugh as Grace passed, a date that wouldn't take no for an answer, some knew. Chastity refused to be shamed. Grace silently watched as she teased up her hair, put on gaudy make up and went out with all the wrong sort of boys. "What?" Chastity shouted in her face. "Why not? They all think it anyway."

Grace's dad broke down the locked bathroom door finding Chastity's body, a lifeless heap wedged where she had fallen, between the toilet and the wall. A belt tied above her elbow and the syringe was still stuck in her arm. The week of high school graduation and it was too late.

"Sleep well, Sweet Pea," Grace whispered, her lower lip trembling.

Darkness descended on the family. They spoke only the common everyday things. Her mother would retreat into the sewing room and sew. The sewing machine would soon stop and Grace would see her slumped forward, her face in her hands weeping. Her father drank beer and then whiskey, sitting silently in the corner of the living room staring a thousand yards into the night beyond the picture window.

Jeff happily stepped into the sunroom and took a deep breath. He smiled, with a steaming mug of coffee in his hand, smelling of a shower with his sparse wet hair combed back. "Morning, honey," he brightly said. "Such a wonderful day. How are you?"

There was a scratching at the screen door. Jeff let Mabel in.

"Fine." Grace stared out the window at the backyard.

"You alright, Grace?"

"Jeff," she said in a distant voice. "We have to talk."

The smile on Jeff's face faded and he regarded Grace. "Is this about that guy Mike? He stopped calling you a couple weeks ago and hasn't bothered us since." Jeff paused. "Was that who called you last night?"

"No," Grace answered, looking down at her hands. "That was a reporter. Sit down, Jeff."

He pulled out a wicker chair and slowly sat. "A reporter?" Jeff gripped his coffee cup tightly in both hands.

"Michael is dead," Grace said, swallowing and sucking in a shuddering breath. "He died in a car accident two weeks ago."

Mabel lay on her pillow near the table, her chin on her outstretched paws. Her dark eyes looked upward from Jeff to Grace and back to Jeff.

"That's too bad." Little sympathy sounded in Jeff's voice. "What did the reporter want?"

"That's what I need to talk to you about." Grace turned and gazed at him for a moment. "Do you love me, Jeff?"

"Of course I do, why?"

"Not like those times I forget my keys in the front door, or can't find my glasses when they are on my head or if I'm scatterbrained and tell you to go to the store as you come in with a bag of groceries."

"Oh, Hon, that's nothing." Jeff eased his grip on the mug, took a drink and smiled.

"What if you knew something terrible happened to me a long time ago?"

"Yes," Jeff reached out for her hand, but stopped.

"And if it was in the newspapers for everyone to read?"

Jeff's smile slowly fell.

The bells of St. Peters tolled, as dark clothed mourners filed out of the chapel following the casket into the cemetery grounds.

A gentle rain beat a sullen tattoo on the polished lid of the coffin borne on the shoulders of the living. Solemn, they marched with a hesitation step: Becky's brother, Mike's two uncles and his best man Mark Larch, Becky's Uncle Wiggly and his nephew Sammie. Mrs. Devereux, Spencer and a petite Japanese girl trailed the casket-bearers. Conveyed by heavy hearts, the coffin itself lay light on the bearers' shoulders. After the horrible accident on I-

80, and the twisted and burnt out wreckage, little remained of Mike Smith to put in the casket.

The young pastor wearing a double breasted black cassock, in the Anglican style walked alongside Mrs. Devereux. He held an umbrella in one hand and bible in the other. Openly sobbing, Mrs. Devereux wore a black frock with long black veil.

"This is the worst year of my life since my husband died," she had confessed to Spencer. "I lost my sweet Rebecca. Now I've lost Mike as well."

'They weren't lost, grandma," Spencer replied. "They were taken from us."

Sheltered from the rain, in a copse of good Norwegian wood, a small, stooped, white-haired man in clear plastic Macintosh over a blue pinstripe suit, wearing a Boss of the Plains hat, watched with no expression as the rain dappled coffin passed.

Slowly, paced to the pealing of the bells, the procession crossed the cemetery. Bill More held hands with his wife Edie as they accompanied Rich Rice and his wife Giselle. Among the mourners were people from the Rockford Call Center and Mike's office in West Des Moines. Others in the cemetery turned and bowed their heads as the coffin went by.

"O God," the pastor's sermon had started, "...who gave us birth...you are ever more ready to hear than we are to pray..." All rose to sing "on the wings of an eagle...in the palm of his hand." And they sat.

"Jesus said I am the resurrection and the life. The one who believes in me will live, even though they die; and whoever lives by believing in me, will never die. In the name of the father, the son and the holy spirit."

The bells stopped, echoing into the distance, as the casket bearers arrived at the grave site. Mourners collected about the Devereux family plot and Mike's final rest next to his beloved Becky. Rain drops tapped on the stretched black cloth of umbrellas.

"I don't want it," Spencer firmly told his grandmother. "My mother and father should be together...forever."

Mrs. Devereux needed no persuading. In fact, she had decided Mike would lie where he belonged. Staggered, reaching out for Spencer's arm the indomitable older woman seemed broken and frail. "I've never cried as much as I have these last months."

As the casket bearers lifted and lowered the coffin to straps above the grave, a cluster of umbrellas pressed closer. Looking around, Bill caught sight of Grace standing on the fringe of the mourners. She had no umbrella. Rain soaked her hair and plastered it to the side of her face. The first part of the Decker investigation would be out in Thursday's newspaper. Bill nudged Rich. Their eyes met. He gave a quick twitch of his head. Rich glanced over and saw Grace. They exchanged surprised looks.

Before rows of flowers, Mrs. Devereux, Spencer and the Japanese girl sat. The largest floral arrangement bore a white silk banner in Rich High green lettering: The Lord Must've Needed a Third Baseman—Decker Real Estate. A smaller circle of flowers next to this was signed from Mr. and Mrs. Gary Watson. The pastor stepped into a spot at the head of the casket. The funeral director dismissed the coffin bearers. They disappeared under umbrellas.

"Let us thank the bearers and friends of the family for supporting the Smiths and Devereux' in this their time of grief. It is with the hope of the resurrection..."

Mike's parents had passed away years ago so Mrs. Devereux got the early morning call from the Illinois State Police after Mike's accident. She drove down from Schaumburg to claim the remains, called Spencer in Washington and made all the arrangements for the funeral. Her will held strong until Spencer arrived from Washington. Even the surprise of Spencer bringing his fiancé, Yumi, could not crack her resolve. She fell apart at dinner that first night. Dishes of food no one had any appetite to eat went cold on the table. She and Spencer talked. Wine loosened their tongues and feelings came forth.

"We were starting to get back to normal," Spencer said. "I was upset for a long time that he had mom's casket closed."

"I saw her body," his grandmother said. "It was horrible. I told your dad he did the right thing. He..." she paused. "He and I agreed. We did not want that to be your last memory of your mother. We wanted you to remember our Becky as tall, confident, beautiful and smart."

"I understand it better now."

"I wasn't a very good mother-in-law to your father. I said a lot of unkind things to him and treated him as if he wasn't good enough for Becky."

"I don't think dad thought that." Spencer lied. Yumi shot him a look.

"Thanks. I know how I treated your father." Mrs. Devereux sighed. "I didn't like him traveling all the time to those dangerous places. I called him names to shame him to better himself. The truth is he was a wonderful husband. I couldn't have hoped for a better man for my daughter. Becky loved him with all her heart. "

"They hardly ever argued, grandma. They'd disagree and talk about it. Then Mom would poke dad in the ribs. He'd laugh and retaliate by pinching her. She'd squirm free and slap his butt. He'd tickle her. They'd wrestle, giggling like teenagers. I'd find them in the kitchen making out..." Spencer trailed off. Yumi's small hand brushed hair off his forehead.

"He loved her. He wasn't the same after her murder."

"Dad knew this would happen. He tried to tell me the last time we talked."

"Nonsense."

"No. He said he was involved in something, well...dangerous."

"I still don't believe it."

"Regardless," Spencer said. "There are two reporters here." He nodded to the mourners. "They asked to talk to me after the service."

"Dreary people dragging our family through the mud ."

"No, I don't think that's it. They said the police also want to contact me."

"Police?" she scoffed. "They can't find the monsters that murdered my daughter, your mother. What do they want? A bribe?"

At the grave side the pastor began. "Today we gather to lay to rest the earthly remains of Michael Clark Smith. Michael was taken to the bosom of the Lord by traffic and mischance. Not more than eight months ago we gathered in this very spot to lay to rest Michael's beloved wife Rebecca. Now, in the arms of the lord, Michael and Rebecca are reunited in the kingdom of heaven for all eternity..."

Under the leafy spruce canopy, the man in the Boss of Plains hat watched the casket cranked into the earth, while Mrs. Devereux gently wept.

"We have renounced disgraceful, underhanded ways. We refuse to practice cunning or tamper with the word of God. But, by the open statement of truth we will commend ourselves to conscience of all in the sight of God."

"Amen," mourners quietly intoned. One by one, couple by couple, they lined up; hugging Mrs. Devereux, shaking Spencer's hand while expressing their deepest sympathies.

Grace stayed back, waiting until nearly all were gone. She approached Spencer.

"I am so sorry about your father." Her wet hair lay matted. Drops of rain, or maybe tears from swollen red eyes, rolled down her reddish cheeks.

Spencer looked at her a moment. "Forgive me... I don't know who you are."

"I knew your dad a long time ago...in high school. He is...was a good man." Grace quickly turned away.

-14-

The story came out in the Thursday afternoon edition of the Park Forest Daily both online and in print. The Friday morning edition of the Chicago Tribune picked it up. The headline read: State Official, Local Mogul in Sex Scandal; with a sub head: Auto Accident Investigation Reopened. Rich Rice and Bill More shared the byline, but it was mostly Rich's writing. He couldn't resist the lead: Dead men tell no tales...or so the guilty hope.

Two large photos were featured under the headline; the first was Sam Decker shaking hands, smiling and receiving an award for Illinois Humanitarian of the year, with inset photos of Rod Decker, Donnie Inge's mug shot and Gary Watson's bank publicity photo. The second photo showed the tangled and charred wreckage of Mike's car on the shoulder of I-80 with an inset photo of the bloody notebook.

Rich sat at his desk typing from notes and finalizing the follow up article on the Decker story. He had denials from Sam Decker, Rod Decker and a refusal to comment from Gary Watson. Donnie Inge cussed him out every time he called. Reporters walked by and patted him on his shoulder, quietly saying "Good story, Rich." He nodded "thanks" knowing he had just received the highest compliment a reporter could get in the newsroom. Bill worked at his computer in his office.

Phones rang, people talked and moved about the newsroom like any other day at the Park Forest Daily.

At lunch, Rich and Bill ate sandwiches in Bill's office, talking casually.

"Sales still won't talk to me," Bill half chuckled. "Can't say I blame them, Decker Real Estate was three to five pages every week." He took a sip from the straw in his drink. "Legal keeps saying: Are you sure? And I think the Trib is going to take over the story."

"I figured that. Hope they let me work on it," Rich said, his mouth full. "The rumor is the Feds are interested."

"Probably," Bill dusted off his fingers. "They were kidnapped."

A commotion could be heard out in the newsroom, loud voices and bright lights flashing and a gang of TV news reporters and cameramen were suddenly crowding around the doorway to Bill's office.

Rich wore a twisted smile on his face as he lounged on the couch in the office. But Bill's mouth and eyes were wide open.

"Yo, Bill!" Rich made a motion around his mouth with his finger. Bill took a paper napkin and wiped his mouth.

"How many girls did they rape?" A reporter yelled, pushing a microphone with WGN on it into the office.

"Do you think they had the Smith guy from Des Moines killed?" A WBBM reporter called out, with a handheld recorder.

"How long were they kidnapping and raping these girls?" another screamed into the office.

"How old was the youngest?"

"Are there witnesses?" a woman from WMAQ shouted.

Bill stood behind his desk with his hands up. "Settle down, folks. Come in and set up and we'll answer all your questions." The reporters filed in and set up lights and sighted in video cameras. "This is Rich Rice, the reporter that wrote the story."

Reporters turned on Rich, who hadn't sat up from his sprawl on the couch.

"How did you uncover this story?"

"Where did you get the information?" Two reporters shouted at once.

"Mr. More, senior editor of the Park Forest Daily," Rich said, motioning toward Bill, who rolled his eyes, but straightened up when the cameras swung on him, "will answer all your questions." Rich's phone started buzzing, loudly. He looked down at the screen.

"The information that led to our investigation was provided by a source outside the newspaper."

"Was that Mike Smith?"

"The guy that died in the accident?"

"Yes," Bill replied. "Mr. Smith provided key information that prompted our looking into the matter and subsequent reporting on it."

"Smith died in a drunk driving accident. Have they reopened the investigation?"

Rich, still staring down at his phone, rose from the couch and with a quick mumbled, "excuse me," shouldered his way out. Reporters flicked glances as he slipped out. Some looked around and caught Rich hurrying out the newsroom and out the front door.

"Can we see the bloody notebook?"

"No, I'm sorry you can't." Bill said. "That has been set aside as state's evidence."

"Where was he going?"

"Can you hold it up so we can get some pictures."

"I don't think you heard me. I don't have it."

Mobile phones started buzzing in the reporter's pockets. They all checked their phones.

"FBI vans just arrived at Sam Decker's house," a reporter whispered. The lights switched off and as quickly as they had descended, the TV reporters were out of the newsroom. One reporter lingered and went over to Bill at his desk. Under his breath he asked, "Can you give me names of some of the girls these guys raped?"

"No way," Bill said emphatically. "Get the hell out of here." The reporter shrugged and trailed after the rest of the group.

-15-

Grace had been dreading a Grand Jury summons since the Park Forest Daily and Tribune stories came out. Once TV picked up the reports about the Sam Decker investigation, she knew she would be called to testify. Jeff drove her downtown the day of her deposition. He had listened and taken Grace's explanation better than she thought he would. He had quiet moments since and she would catch him looking at her, differently.

The Dan Ryan Expressway brought back memories of the day long ago when she did it. She had been so afraid after the rape, afraid it would be found out and she would be publicly humiliated. She was afraid her parents would find out. Her mother would become angry and beat her. Her father would be silent, filled with shame. He'd never meet her gaze, nor look upon her in the same loving light as he once had for his eldest daughter. And they said they would kill her parents. She missed her period the first month. A greater fear began gnawing at her. Perhaps it was just anxiety she told herself over and over, day upon day, as each night she cried herself to sleep. She missed a second month and she knew.

Unable to sleep, Grace turned it over in her mind all night long, what to do, what to do, again and again. "I'm so scared," she whispered, between the tears. "Help me, please." She prayed, constantly.

Chastity, angry and bitter, told Grace to have the baby and put Decker on the birth certificate as the father.

Grace couldn't have the baby. She was in high school. She wouldn't be able to hide her pregnancy. People in town would find out. She had no place to go.

She took the handful of aspirin and lay down on her bed. Around midnight she started vomiting. Her mother came rushing in to her bedside. Yellow vomit with undigested white pills splashed across the bedspread and the floor.

"Are you okay, Grace?" she asked anxiously.

"I'm sick, mom."

"I'll get a cold compress." Her mother stood.

Grace's father leaned on the door in his pajamas. "Is she alright?" he said, yawning.

"She's fine," Grace's mother replied, pushing past him.

She returned with a towel, glass of water, compress and closed the door behind her. Putting the compress gently on Grace's forehead, brushing back the hair from the side of her face, she softly asked, "Is it about that boy, that Mike?"

"No, mom," Grace struggled to answer. "It's not about Michael."

She smiled and stroked Grace's cheek. "Oh now, sweetie, I'm not such an old fogey that I don't remember how much it hurts when a boy breaks your heart." She became serious. "But this is not the way to handle it." There was a hint of anger in her tone.

Grace started to retch. Her mother tossed the towel in front of her. She seemed impatient. "Do you know how other people would look at us if you had succeeded?"

"I'm...I'm sorry, mother," Grace managed to say.

"You're damn right you're sorry. If you ever try anything this stupid again you'll get a hiding like you've never had." She rose from the bed. "Now clean up this mess."

Morning traffic on the Dan Ryan shunted along with Jeff growing more and more frustrated. "Come on. Come on," he muttered.

Chastity got her new boyfriend to drive them into Chicago that morning. She had started going with older boys, the ones with cars. This one was named Danny, or Don, or Dave, Grace couldn't concentrate. The radio played low, Fleetwood Mac, as Grace stared out the passenger window watching the cars, houses and buildings pass. Every once in a while she caught her own reflection in the glass and turned away. Chastity sat next to her boyfriend, chatting nonstop, playing with his long hair, asking him over and over if he liked her. Almost 15 years old, as cute as Lolita, Chastity now had a reputation the opposite of her name.

Grace had nearly cleaned out her bank account and college fund, money saved from years of baby-sitting. She used some of the money for a fake ID supplied by another of Chastity's older boyfriends.

"There's the exit, Denny," Chastity pointed, then reached under his T-shirt and pinched his nipple.

"Ouch," he laughed, swerving the beat up car and exiting the Dan Ryan. "Hey, are you sure this is where we're going? I thought it was the museum."

"Later," Chastity said. "We have to make a stop first. Take a left."

"A left?" he said. "This is not a real good place." Denny looked around at the south side neighborhood.

"What's the address Grace?" Grace did not respond. Chastity gave her a nudge.

"What?" Grace said, coming out of a fog.

"The address? What's the address of the place?"

Grace opened her fist and smoothed out the crumpled piece of paper on her thigh. "It's on Marshfield Street. The Back of the Yards family clinic."

At a stop light Denny stared at a group of young black men loitering around the entrance to a liquor store. He looked at the light, tapping his fingers nervously on the steering wheel. "Make sure the windows are up and doors locked, okay?" he said tensely. "We're on the wrong side of the Dan Ryan."

They found the clinic. It was an old two story black and white tile structure with a large window of opaque glass bricks, narrow barred door topped with an arched window.

"There it is." Grace pointed.

"Pull into that lot," Chastity said.

They pulled into an alleyway parking lot.

"Hey," Denny asked. "What's going on here?"

"Shut up, Denny." Chastity slapped his shoulder. She looked at Grace. "Do you have the ID?"

"Yes," Grace started to cry.

"What's your name?"

Grace fumbled in her purse and got the ID card. "It's Kimberly Novacek," she replied, choking back tears.

"You have the money?"

"Yes," Grace stuttered. "Come with me, Chas, please."

There was a moment of silence.

"Okay," Chastity said. "Denny you wait for us here. It might be an hour."

"An hour?" he protested.

Chastity grabbed a handful of his T-shirt. "If you're not here when we come out I will tell everybody how tiny your dick is."

"Alright," he relented. "God, it still smells like the stockyards out here."

They clung to each other as they walked to the front of the clinic. Grace couldn't stop weeping, nor could she stop remembering the night they were pushed out of the car at the shopping center parking lot. There were single women, Hispanic and black women with children in the large white tile waiting room. A baby wailed. People talked loud. Clouds of blue cigarette smoke drifted through the room. They waited in line and after a few minutes went up to a heavy black woman dressed in whites like a nurse, sitting behind a thick Plexiglas window. The window was smeared with handprints and stained with brown grime at the corners.

"Do you have an appointment?" she asked in a bored tone.

Grace froze.

"Do you have an appointment?" she repeated slower and above the noise.

"Y-yes," she finally managed to answer, speaking into a vented stainless steel circle in the middle of the Plexiglas window.

"Your name?"

Again Grace froze.

"Come on, Kim," Chastity said, giving Grace a shake. "The nurse doesn't have all day." Then as an aside to the nurse, said, "She's a little nervous."

"It's Kimberly Novacek," Grace read off the ID card. The card shook in her hand.

"You been crying, honey? How old are you?" the nurse asked suspiciously.

"I'm," Grace glanced at the card and did some quick math. "I'm 19 years old."

"May I see your ID please," the nurse reached out through the small open space under the Plexiglas and snatched the ID card from Grace's shaking hand. She looked at it a long moment, then back at Grace. "You're rushing your birthday, girl. This says you're still 18 years old. Child, that picture is very unflattering." The nurse glanced at the appointment sheet on her desk. "Yes, I see your name here, Novacek. You are scheduled for...." She paused, her head tilted, regarding Grace. "...for a procedure with Dr. Jamison. Do you have medical insurance?"

"No," Grace blurted out.

"How do you plan to pay for the procedure?"

"Cash." Grace reached into her purse. "They told me it would be five hundred dollars." She pulled out a fat envelope of wrinkled and worn green bills in different denominations. "It's all there."

"Uh huh." The nurse took the envelope and studied Grace a long time. "Were you referred by your family doctor?

"No."

"So how do you know you," the nurse hesitated, "need a procedure?"

"I know."

"When was your last period?" the nurse asked.

"More than two and a half months ago."

"So you missed two cycles," the nurse made a note, then asked, "Have you talked to your parents?"

Startled by the question Grace didn't respond.

"She's over 18 years old," Chastity answered curtly.

"Have you spoken to a clergyman?" the nurse added.

"Look, nurse," Chastity said impatiently. "She's over 18 and the law says she can get this taken care of."

"Back off, girly," the nurse said, sliding a clip board and pen, with Grace's ID, under the Plexiglas. "Fill this out and bring it with you when you're called." The nurse shot Chastity a withering look, then put the envelope in a lower drawer. "Next please."

Tightly holding each other, Grace and Chastity walked to the waiting area and two chairs in the corner.

"I don't want to do this anymore," Grace whispered. "Let's go."

"No way," Chastity said. "Fill that out."

Trembling, Grace filled in the form and they waited. Chastity kept up a monologue whispered in Grace's ear about the clinic and people in the waiting room. "Can you please shut that kid up? This place is really dirty. She's got to have 10 kids and looks like she's about to pop out an 11th. Wow, that chick has nothing but gold teeth. It does smell like the stockyards in here. That can't be her real hair color. Speaking of butts, it looks like she's dragging two elephants behind her. Some people shouldn't be allowed to wear tight clothes. Maybe you should lose about 100 pounds, lady."

"Novacek?" a short Hispanic woman wearing thick black glasses called into the waiting area. She stood by a white door leading into the examination rooms.

Grace didn't move. Chastity looked at her.

"Novacek?"

"Gracie," Chastity said seriously. "If you don't want to do this...we can go."

Hearing Chastity say that gave Grace resolve. "No," she said, standing. "Let's take care of this."

Jeff vented a sharp sigh and snapped Grace back to reality. Expressway traffic had let up and he could maintain a pace without tapping his brakes every few minutes. "We'll be there on time," he said reassuringly, patting Grace's knee. She caught his smile in a quick glance and smiled back.

They parked in a garage on Dearborn Street. Grace clutched Jeff's arm tightly as they walked across the busy city street to the tall red and brown Richard J. Daley Center adjacent to the grey stone and tall Greek columns of city hall. A flock of pigeons took flight as they passed.

"I'm not looking forward to this, Jeff."

"Hon, just go in and tell them everything that happened, just like you told it to me." He gently stroked her arm. "You'll be fine. I'm right here for you."

"Please don't be mad at me, Jeff, I can't stop thinking about Michael." She looked down and added softly, "And Chastity."

"It's alright," he replied.

She caught sight of the Picasso construct in front of the building. "Why do they let it rust like that?"

"Maybe someone should slap a coat of municipal orange on it?"

They pushed through the heavy glass doors and crossed to a grey mottled marble counter staffed with uniformed security. Grace showed the summons to an officer. He said "Room 500, Fifth floor" in a flat tone and handed back the summons, pointing them to the security screening. They looked through Grace's purse and patted down Jeff, then motioned them through to the elevators. Grace and Jeff stepped into the elevator, pressed 5 and shuffled to the back. Another couple slipped into the front of the elevator as the doors started to close. Grace looked at the woman. She was fidgety, obviously nervous, with a tissue balled in her fist.

They waited until the elevator emptied on the fifth floor then stepped out and hung back. The other couple went down the wide, marble hallway ahead of them. The sound of their hushed voices and heels echoed off the polished stone walls. Jeff put both his hands on her shoulders. "You're shaking. It will be fine, Grace."

"I'm scared."

A uniformed woman officer, seated at a table by the entrance to Room 500, asked Grace her name.

"Grace Jordan."

The officer leafed through a stack of sheets clipped to a clipboard. "I don't see Grace Jordan. Is that your maiden name?"

"Oh, I'm sorry. It's House, Grace House."

"Okay," the officer said slowly, checking off a name on the sheet. "Go into the room. They will call you when it's time for you to testify."

"Can I go in?" Jeff asked, not letting go of Grace's arm.

"Yes, you can," the officer answered, with a wave over her shoulder.

"Thank you," Grace said, opening the door and stepping into the room. She stopped, surprised. There must have been between 30 to 40 people in the waiting room, some seated, some in groups, some alone, some standing along the wall and others quietly talking. Grace saw couples and many single women ranging from very young to middle-aged. Looking around Grace recalled Michael's comment that she and Chastity were likely not the only ones the Deckers had raped. She realized he'd been right.

Across the room a woman caught Grace's eye. She weaved through the crowd in short, tight steps. Grace's age, the woman's eye makeup had smeared with teary streaks. Grace's mouth opened. She glanced up to Jeff and then to the woman.

"Oh my god, that's Rachel from high school."

The two women hugged.

"I am so sorry, Grace," she broke down and sobbed. "I knew. I knew all through high school they did the same thing to you and your sister they did to me. We shared a horrible secret. I was afraid, afraid if they found out-- everyone would talk about me."

"It's okay, Rachel," Grace reassured her. "It's all over now."

"Is it? Is it ever over?"

ABOUT THE AUTHOR

Photo by Torri Pantaleon

Cort Fernald is a professional writer with newspaper and magazine publishing credits spanning more than 30 years. Cort has written news, features and editorials for a variety of publications.

In 2013 Cort published his first novel *Algonquin*. *Algonquin* is available through Amazon.com. *Sisters' Secret* is his second novel.

Cort has a degree in English from Southern Oregon University, and did graduate work in journalism at the University of Oregon. A member of the Nebraska Writers Workshop, Cort currently resides in Omaha, Nebraska.

AlGONQUIN by Cort Fernald

When Royce Partridge learns his boyhood pal Toby Bergman is dying of cancer he returns to the small town of Algonquin, Illinois on the Fox River where they grew up. Royce left Algonquin 40 years ago. Progress in the form of strip malls, subdivisions and congested traffic, has changed the once bucolic river town. Royce surprises Toby in the hospital and slipping fast. Royce stays in Algonquin at a quaint Victorian bed & breakfast.

Despite of the heavy hand of progress Royce can see the small town he and Toby raced mopeds around as teenagers. But it is down on the banks of the Fox River that Royce relives the wild adventure he, Toby and two other friends had the summer of 1964 before they started high school.

Available on Amazon.com and Amazon kindle.

www.ingramcontent.com/pod-product-compliance
Lightning Source LLC
Chambersburg PA
CBHW070325130626
46556CB00007B/2731